THE ORPHAN'S LETTERS TO PROVIDENCE

RACHEL DOWNING

CORNERSTONETALES.COM

A GLORIOUS MORNING

The sun rose gently over the Yorkshire landscape, painting the modest parsonage in hues of amber and gold. Light filtered through the thin curtains of Alice's small bedroom, casting dancing patterns across her eyelids. She stirred beneath her blanket, the familiar sounds of morning birds coaxing her from slumber.

Alice opened her eyes, blinking away the remnants of sleep. Eleven years old and already accustomed to the rhythm of early mornings, she took a moment to appreciate the quiet stillness before the day began in earnest. The wooden floorboards creaked beneath her as she stretched her limbs, feeling the pleasant ache of growing bones.

With practiced movements, Alice slipped from her bed and reached for the simple brown dress hanging on the hook by her wardrobe. The fabric was worn at the elbows, but clean and carefully mended. She dressed quickly, fingers deftly doing up the buttons before tying her apron around her waist. The apron had once been white but now bore the faint shadows of countless meals prepared and surfaces cleaned.

In the small kitchen, Alice moved with quiet efficiency. She stoked the dying embers in the stove, adding kindling until flames licked upward. The porridge oats went into the pot with water and a pinch of salt—no milk today, as they'd run out yesterday. As she stirred, Alice softly sang "Rock of Ages," her father's favourite hymn, her young voice clear in the morning quiet.

"That's a fine tune to greet the day with."

Alice turned to find her father standing in the doorway. Reverend Thomas Wells' salt-and-pepper hair stood slightly ruffled, as if he'd run his fingers through it while pondering some theological question before coming downstairs.

"Good morning, Father." Alice smiled, continuing to stir the thickening porridge.

"You've become quite the little housekeeper." He crossed the room and placed a gentle hand on her shoulder. "Your mother would be proud of how you've grown."

Alice's heart warmed at the rare mention of her mother. She ladled the porridge into two bowls and placed them on the small wooden table where they took their meals.

"Mrs Pemberton's youngest has the croup," Reverend Wells said between spoonfuls. "I thought we might visit them this morning, bring some of that honey from Mr Thompson."

"The Pembertons live near the mill, don't they?" Alice asked, her interest piqued. "Will we see the workers changing shifts?"

Her father nodded. "Indeed. Though I worry for those children. Some a bit younger than you, working such long hours in dangerous conditions."

"Is that why you spoke about the Good Samaritan in Sunday's sermon? Because of the mill children?"

Reverend Wells looked at his daughter with surprised appreciation. "You've a keen mind, Alice. Yes, I believe our Christian duty extends to all neighbours, especially those most vulnerable. Mr Pullman didn't seem to appreciate the message, however."

"But it was from Scripture," Alice reasoned, her brow furrowed in thought. "Surely he cannot argue with the Lord's teachings?"

"Men find ways to interpret God's word to suit their purposes." Her father sighed. "But that doesn't make it right."

SIMPLE KINDNESS

Alice helped her father clear away the breakfast things, her movements mirroring his with practiced ease. They'd shared this morning ritual for as long as she could remember, and there was comfort in its familiarity.

"We should take something for the Pembertons," she suggested, reaching for the cloth-lined basket they used for parish visits. "Perhaps some of yesterday's bread? Along with Mr Thompson's honey might soothe the little one's throat."

Her father nodded approvingly. "Excellent thought, Alice. Kindness in small measures often brings the greatest comfort."

Alice wrapped the half-loaf carefully in a clean cloth, placing it gently in the basket alongside the small jar of honey. She paused, her fingers hovering over the basket's contents.

"Father, might we cut some flowers from the garden? The daffodils are particularly fine this year."

"A splash of sunshine for a sickroom—yes, indeed."

As her father fetched his worn leather Bible, Alice slipped outside to the modest garden that surrounded the parsonage. She selected blooms with care—bright yellow daffodils, delicate bluebells, and a sprig of lavender for its soothing scent. The morning dew still clung to the petals, catching the light like tiny diamonds.

"Oh, Father," she called as she returned inside, arranging the flowers atop their offerings. "We mustn't forget Mrs Wellings. Her rheumatism has been troubling her terribly. She mentioned it when I helped with the church flowers on Saturday."

Her father's eyes crinkled with warm regard. "What a thoughtful soul you are. Mrs Wellings would certainly welcome a visit. We shall make time for her too."

With their basket prepared, they set out along the village path. Alice's small hand found its place naturally within her father's larger one. The morning had bloomed into full glory now, birds darting overhead with cheerful songs.

"Look there, Father!" Alice pointed to where wild primroses dotted the hedgerow. "Aren't they lovely? Like tiny pieces of sunshine nestled in the green."

"God's handiwork is evident in even the smallest bloom," Reverend Wells replied, his voice taking on the gentle cadence Alice recognised from his most thoughtful moments. "Just as His compassion shows itself in our smallest acts of kindness."

They walked in companionable silence for a few paces before he continued, "You know, Alice, true charity isn't merely giving what we can spare. It's giving what might cost us something—our time, our comfort, perhaps even our reputation among certain folk."

Alice nodded, absorbing his words. "Like when you spoke against the conditions at the mill, even though Mr Pullman was displeased?"

"Precisely so. Sometimes the most Christian act is to stand firm when others would have us look away from suffering."

Alice's heart lifted at the sight of the Pembertons' cottage, its thatched roof and stone walls standing sturdy against the morning light. As her father knocked gently on the weathered door, it swung open to reveal Mrs Pemberton, her face drawn with worry yet brightening at their arrival.

"Reverend Wells, Miss Alice, bless you both for coming," she said, ushering them inside.

The moment Alice crossed the threshold, the sweet, comforting scent of lavender enveloped her. Bundles hung from the ceiling beams, filling the modest home with their soothing fragrance.

"We've brought some things that might help little Thomas," Alice said, presenting their basket. Mrs Pemberton's eyes welled with grateful tears as she accepted the honey and bread.

"The flowers are lovely too. Perhaps they'll cheer him," Alice added softly.

They spent a tender hour with the Pembertons, her father reading passages of comfort while Alice sat beside the feverish child, cooling his brow with a damp cloth. When they finally took their leave, Alice felt that peculiar mixture of sadness and purpose that always accompanied their parish visits.

The walk to Mrs Wellings' cottage took them past the churchyard. Alice's gaze lingered on her mother's headstone, as it always did, before they continued on their way.

Mrs Wellings greeted them with trembling hands and rheumy eyes. Her cottage was neat but sparse, the emptiness speaking of her solitude since Mr Wellings had passed three winters ago.

"These are for you," Alice said, presenting the remaining flowers she'd gathered that morning. "The daffodils from our garden are particularly bright this year."

Mrs Wellings' face transformed, joy erasing the deep lines of pain that usually marked her features. "Oh, my dear child, how thoughtful you are. They're beautiful."

"Thank you for your kindness," she added, her gnarled fingers gently touching the delicate petals.

When her father knelt to pray, Alice joined him without

hesitation, her small knees pressing against the worn rug. As Reverend Wells spoke words of comfort and hope, Alice felt the weight of their shared faith settle around them like a warm blanket.

After the prayer, Alice took Mrs Wellings' hands in her own. "Would you tell me about when you were a girl? What games did you play in springtime?"

Mrs Wellings' eyes brightened with remembered joy. "Oh, we'd make daisy chains and race hoops down the lane. And the May Day celebrations! The ribbons and dancing..."

As the elderly woman's stories flowed, Alice listened with genuine interest, asking questions that drew out even more colourful memories.

Her father sat quietly nearby, occasionally adding a thoughtful comment or gentle laugh. Alice caught his gaze once —the pride in his eyes warming her from within. In these moments, she understood what it truly meant to minister to others, not just through scripture and prayer, but through the simple gift of presence and attention.

OBSERVATIONS

After leaving Mrs Wellings' cottage, Alice walked beside her father in companionable silence. The late afternoon sun cast long shadows across the path, and Alice found herself contemplating the day's visits. She glanced up at her father's profile, noticing how the golden light softened the lines around his eyes.

"You have a gift, Alice," he said suddenly, breaking the quiet. "The way you spoke with Mrs Wellings—drawing out her stories, making her feel truly heard. That's ministry in its purest form."

Alice felt warmth bloom in her chest at his words. To be useful to her father in his work meant everything to her.

"I simply enjoy listening to her," she replied, tucking a stray lock of hair behind her ear. "Her stories make the past feel alive."

"That's precisely it. You see people, truly see them." He squeezed her hand. "Your mother had that same gift."

As twilight descended, they took their customary detour through the churchyard. Gravestones cast long shadows across the grass, and the evening air carried the scent of wild roses that climbed the ancient stone wall.

"Father," Alice ventured, "why does God allow some to suffer more than others? The Pembertons work so hard, yet little Thomas falls ill. Mrs Wellings lives alone with her pain."

Reverend Wells considered her question carefully. "The distribution of suffering is one of faith's great mysteries. We cannot always understand God's purpose, but we can be His instruments of comfort."

They stopped before a simple headstone, weathered but well-tended. *Eleanor Wells, Beloved Wife and Mother, Called Home to God's Embrace.* Alice knelt to brush away a fallen leaf.

"Your mother faced each day with extraordinary courage," her father said softly. "Even knowing her confinement might be dangerous, she embraced the joy of bringing you into this world. She believed firmly that love must triumph over fear."

Alice traced the engraved letters with her fingertip. "Would she be pleased with me, do you think?"

"Beyond measure." His voice caught slightly. "She would see, as I do, how you embody her compassionate spirit."

They settled on a bench overlooking the church, its spire silhouetted against the deepening purple sky. The first stars appeared, pinpricks of light in the vast expanse.

"What are your thoughts on God tonight, Alice?" her father asked, his tone gentle but curious.

Alice considered, watching a nightjar swoop low across the graves. "I think perhaps God speaks to us through beauty as much as through Scripture. The primroses this morning, Mrs Wellings' smile when I gave her the daffodils—these seem like divine messages too."

Her father nodded, his expression thoughtful. "A profound observation. God reveals Himself in countless ways to those attentive enough to notice."

"I want to learn more," Alice said, her voice gaining conviction. "About Scripture, yes, but also about how to truly help people. Like you do."

Back at the parsonage, Alice lit the lamps while her father organized his notes for tomorrow's sermon. She fetched his spectacles from the study and placed them beside his Bible, taking quiet pleasure in these small acts of service.

Later, nestled in bed with her journal open before her, Alice wrote by candlelight:

Dear Journal,

Today we visited the Pembertons and Mrs Wellings. I cooled Thomas's brow while Father read from Psalms. Mrs Wellings told me about May Day celebrations when she was young—her eyes shone with remembered joy.

Father says I have Mother's gift for seeing people. I hope this is true. I find that listening is a form of prayer—a way of honoring the divine spark in others.

The primroses along the hedgerow were like tiny suns. Perhaps beauty is God's way of reminding us He is present, even in suffering.

Tomorrow is Sunday. I shall help Father prepare his vestments before the service.

Alice closed her journal and blew out her candle. The moonlight filtered through her curtains, casting patterns across her quilt. She thought of her mother, of Mrs. Wellings' gnarled hands, of little Thomas' feverish brow. Each person a world of experiences, each one precious. With this comforting thought, she drifted into sleep, secure in the knowledge of her place in this small corner of Yorkshire—daughter, helper, apprentice in compassion.

THE MILL

The textile mill dominated the village skyline, its brick chimney belching thick smoke that hung like a pall over the rooftops. The rhythmic thrum of machinery pulsed through the air, a heartbeat so different from the gentle quiet of the Wells parsonage. Alice paused on the hilltop path, watching as the massive structure swallowed the morning light, its windows reflecting nothing back but darkness despite the day's brightness.

The factory bell rang, signalling the end of one shift. Alice watched as workers spilled from the narrow doorways, a stream of hunched figures moving like weary ants. Children as young as seven or eight stumbled alongside adults, their small frames dwarfed by the building they'd spent twelve hours inside. A girl no older than Alice herself passed by, cotton fluff caught in her hair, her fingers stained blue from the dyes. Their eyes met briefly—the girl's gaze hollow, lacking the spark that should animate a child's face.

In the village square, Alice lingered by the greengrocer's stall, pretending to examine apples while straining to hear the conversation between Mrs Hargrove and the butcher's wife.

"The reverend's treading dangerous ground with his sermons," Mrs. Hargrove whispered, though not quietly enough. "Mr Pullman was in a right state after Sunday service. Said it wasn't a minister's place to meddle in business matters."

"Pullman's got half the parish council in his pocket," replied the butcher's wife, glancing nervously around. "Mark my words, he'll not stand for being called unchristian before his own workers."

Alice clutched her basket tighter, the weight of their words heavier than the bread and vegetables inside.

At home, she found her father in his study, surrounded by books and papers. Sunlight slanted through the window, illuminating dust motes that danced around his bent head. His spectacles had slipped down his nose as he scribbled notes, pausing occasionally to consult his Bible.

"Father?" Alice placed her basket on a chair. "May I help?"

Reverend Wells looked up, his expression softening at the sight of her. "Alice, my dear. Yes, perhaps you can." He gestured to the chair opposite his desk. "I'm struggling with Sunday's message. The plight of those mill children weighs heavily on my heart."

"Mr Pullman won't be pleased," Alice said quietly, remembering the gossip.

"Truth must be spoken, even when unwelcome." Her father removed his spectacles, rubbing the bridge of his nose. "Christ calls us to defend the vulnerable, not accommodate those who exploit them."

Alice nodded, reaching for her father's Bible. "What about the passage from Isaiah? 'Learn to do good; seek justice, correct oppression; bring justice to the fatherless, plead the widow's cause.'"

Her father's eyes brightened. "Perfect. And perhaps paired with James—'faith without works is dead.' We must remind our congregation that Christian charity extends beyond prayer, to action."

OUR DUTY

Sunday morning arrived with a crisp clarity that seemed to sharpen every sound and sight. Alice smoothed her best dress—faded blue cotton that had once been her mother's—and watched as the church filled. The pews creaked under the weight of bodies, a sea of worn faces and calloused hands. Mill workers occupied the front rows, their presence a testament to their faith despite exhaustion etched into their features. Children sat beside parents, some with bandaged fingers, others with the telltale stoop that came from hours bent over machinery.

Alice sat in her usual place, the polished wooden pew worn smooth from years of Wells family occupancy. From here, she could see everyone—the mill workers, the shopkeepers, and in the back corner, Mr Grimsby, Pullman's business manager, his thin lips pressed into a disapproving line.

Her father emerged from the vestry, Bible in hand. Though not a tall man, Reverend Wells commanded attention, his gentle authority filling the small stone church. Sunlight streamed through stained glass, casting jewelled patterns across his face as he opened his Bible.

"'Learn to do good; seek justice, correct oppression,'" he began, his voice clear and unwavering. "Isaiah teaches us that faith requires action. That love—true Christian love—cannot exist alongside injustice."

Alice watched as heads nodded throughout the congregation. Mrs Pemberton, little Thomas recovered but still pale, clutched her husband's hand. Old Thomas the gardener leaned forward on his walking stick, eyes bright with agreement.

"When we allow children—God's most precious gifts—to be worked until their bodies break, we have failed as Christians." Her father's voice grew passionate. "When profit matters more than the wellbeing of innocents, we have strayed from Christ's teachings."

He never mentioned Pullman by name, but his meaning was unmistakable. Alice glanced toward the mill workers. A young woman with hollow cheeks and red-rimmed eyes wiped away tears. Beside her, a man with a bandaged arm nodded fiercely, his expression one of vindication.

"God calls us to courage," Reverend Wells continued. "To stand against those who would build fortunes on the broken backs of children. To speak truth, even when that truth brings discomfort to the powerful."

After the final hymn, parishioners clustered around her father. Alice lingered nearby, arranging hymnals while listening.

"Powerful words, Reverend," whispered Mr Cooper, who worked the looms. "But Pullman won't stand for it. He's already docked wages for those seen nodding during last week's sermon."

"We appreciate your support," added Mrs Finch, whose ten-year-old son had lost two fingers in the carding machine. "But we fear for you."

Alice felt a chill despite the warm spring day. Across the churchyard, she noticed Mr Grimsby in hushed conversation with two parish council members, repeatedly glancing toward her father.

"Faith must guide us in dark times," her father replied, squeezing Mrs Finch's shoulder. "If we abandon truth for comfort, what example do we set for our children?"

~

Alice sat quietly in the back pew of the church, her small hands folded in her lap as she watched the parish council members file into the vestry. Father had asked her to wait while he attended the meeting, promising they would walk home together afterwards. Though he hadn't said so, Alice knew he wanted her nearby—perhaps for his own comfort as much as hers.

The vestry door remained ajar, allowing snippets of conversation to drift into the nave. Alice heard her father's measured tones as he called the meeting to order, followed by the scraping of chairs and clearing of throats.

Then came a sound that made her stomach tighten—heavy footsteps on the stone floor, followed by a sudden hush. Alice rose from her seat and crept closer to the vestry door.

Silas Pullman had entered, his imposing figure filling the doorway before he stepped inside. Though Alice couldn't see him clearly, she could imagine his expression—the same cold stare he'd fixed on her father after Sunday services.

"Gentlemen," Pullman's voice carried clearly. "I trust I'm not interrupting. As the largest employer in the parish, I felt it prudent to attend."

Alice heard her father's chair creak. "Mr Pullman. We welcome all parishioners to council meetings."

The tension in the room seeped through the doorway like a cold draught. Alice pressed herself against the wall beside the door, heart fluttering beneath her ribs.

"I've been hearing troubling reports," Pullman continued, his voice silky yet sharp. "It seems our church has taken a particular interest in matters of business. Specifically, my business."

"The church has always concerned itself with the welfare of its flock," her father replied evenly.

"Indeed. But perhaps the shepherd should tend to spiritual matters rather than... temporal ones. Factory management requires expertise beyond theological training."

Alice bit her lip, recognising the threat beneath Pullman's words. The vestry had gone silent.

"A well-run factory," Pullman continued, "like a well-run parish, requires the right person in charge. Someone who understands their proper place and role. Someone who knows the consequences of... overreaching."

The threat hung in the air. Alice's hands trembled as she pressed them against the cool stone wall.

"Gentlemen," her father's voice remained steady, "our duty to the poor and vulnerable is not a matter of convenience, but of Christian obligation. Opposition, however powerful, cannot deter us from this sacred responsibility."

Alice slipped back to her pew, her heart racing with fear for her father. The vestry door remained ajar, but she could no longer bear to listen.

INJUSTICE

Alice followed her father home from the church in silence, her mind replaying Mr Pullman's veiled threats. The familiar path to the parsonage offered no comfort today; even the evening birdsong seemed muted against her troubled thoughts.

After supper, while her father settled at his desk with parish accounts, Alice approached him. Her fingers twisted the edge of her apron as she stood beside his chair.

"Father," she began, her voice smaller than she intended. "I heard what Mr Pullman said to you. Are we in danger?"

Reverend Wells set down his pen and turned to face her. The lamplight cast deep shadows beneath his eyes, making him appear older than his years.

"Come here, my dear." He patted his knee, and Alice perched there as she had done since childhood. "What troubles you most about what you heard?"

"He threatened you," Alice said plainly. "Because you spoke truth about the children in his mill."

Her father nodded slowly. "Yes, he did. And that is precisely why we must continue to speak."

"But he's powerful. Everyone says so."

"Indeed he is." Reverend Wells took Alice's hand in his. "But remember what I've taught you about Our Lord. When faced with powerful men who abused the vulnerable, did He remain silent?"

Alice shook her head. "No. He challenged them, even when they sought to harm Him."

"Exactly so. And while I pray Mr Pullman will have a change of heart, we cannot abandon those children to their suffering merely because speaking up brings discomfort—or even danger—to ourselves."

Alice considered this, feeling something kindle within her chest—a warmth that pushed against her fear.

"The children at the mill," she said. "They're like the lambs Jesus spoke of, aren't they?"

Her father's eyes brightened with pride. "They are indeed. And we are called to protect them, even against wolves in fine clothing."

Over the following Sundays, Alice noticed more mill workers filling the pews. They came with bandaged hands and weary faces, yet something in their expressions changed as they listened to her father's words. The church had become more than a building—it was becoming a sanctuary where their suffering was acknowledged.

Alice watched them gather after services, speaking in low voices, sharing their stories. She saw how Mrs Stalwart, whose son had lost two fingers in the machinery, found comfort with Mr Davies, whose daughter worked twelve-hour shifts despite her chronic cough.

While arranging hymn sheets the following week, Alice paused, running her fingers over the printed words of "A Mighty Fortress Is Our God." She thought of her father's courage, of the mill children's resilient spirits, of Mr Pullman's cold eyes.

"I'll help you, Father," she whispered to herself. "However I can."

Though anxiety lingered like morning mist over the churchyard, Alice felt something stronger growing alongside it—a determined hope that justice might yet prevail for those who had no voice of their own.

DEVOTION

Dark clouds smothered the Yorkshire sky like a funeral shroud, turning day to premature dusk. Alice pressed her forehead against the cold glass of the parsonage window, watching the first fat raindrops splatter against the pane. At fourteen, she had witnessed many storms, but something about this one twisted her stomach into knots.

"It's coming down rather heavily now," she murmured, more to herself than to anyone else.

The wind howled through the eaves, and the rain transformed from scattered drops to sheets of water cascading from the heavens. Alice's gaze drifted toward the river that curved around the edge of the village. Already, the water lapped dangerously high against its banks, muddy brown and churning with angry purpose.

Behind her, the floorboards creaked. Alice turned to find her father shrugging into his heavy woollen coat, his face set with quiet determination.

"You cannot mean to go out in this," she said, moving away from the window.

Reverend Wells reached for his hat. "Young Jack Finch has

taken a turn for the worse. His mother sent word not an hour ago."

"But Father, look at the river. It's nearly breached its banks already."

"All the more reason for me to go now, before it becomes impassable." He buttoned his coat to the neck, his movements unhurried despite the urgency of his mission. "The boy asked for me specifically. I cannot abandon him when he needs spiritual comfort most."

Alice wrung her hands. "Surely God would understand if you waited until the storm passes."

Her father's expression softened as he placed his hands on her shoulders. "My dear child, do you remember what I told you about our calling? We must go where we are needed, when we are needed—not when it is convenient or safe."

"I know, but—" Alice bit her lip, unable to articulate the dread that settled in her chest like a stone.

"The Finches live in the low cottages by the mill. Mr Pullman specifically requested I visit today." He cupped her cheek with his weathered hand. "I shan't be long. Keep the fire stoked, and perhaps prepare some soup for when I return."

Alice nodded, her throat tight. "Promise you'll be careful."

"I promise." He pressed a kiss to her forehead. "Providence watches over us all."

As he reached for the door, Alice felt a curious mixture of fear and pride. This was who her father was—a man who would wade through floodwaters to bring comfort to a dying child. How could she not admire such devotion, even as it terrified her?

Alice bustled about the parsonage, trying to silence the anxiety that had settled in her chest. She swept the kitchen floor with such vigour that dust clouds rose around her ankles. Every few minutes, she abandoned her chores to peer through the window, watching the rain hammer against the glass with increasing fury. The river had swollen to twice its normal width, swallowing the muddy banks and creeping toward the lowest cottages.

"He should have returned by now," she whispered, her breath fogging the cold pane.

As afternoon dragged into evening, Alice lit the lamps and stoked the fire until it roared in the grate. The flames cast dancing shadows across the walls, but offered little comfort. Unable to concentrate on her usual tasks, she retreated to her father's study and pulled her mother's Bible from its place of honour on the shelf.

The leather binding felt smooth beneath her fingers, worn from years of devoted handling. Alice traced the faded gold lettering, imagining her mother's hands doing the same. She had no memories of Eleanor Wells—only the stories her father shared and this precious book that connected them across the veil of death.

Alice opened to the Psalms, her mother's favourite, according to her father. The pages fell open naturally to the twenty-third Psalm, the margins filled with delicate handwriting. She ran her fingertips over the ink, feeling closer to the woman she'd never known.

"Yea, though I walk through the valley of the shadow of death, I will fear no evil," she read aloud, her voice barely audible above the storm's rage.

Night descended, bringing no relief from the tempest. Alice paced the sitting room, counting her steps between the window and the door, her shadow stretching and contracting with each pass of the fireplace. The wind howled through every crack in the old parsonage, rattling the windows in their frames.

The distant toll of church bells reached her ears—nine, ten, eleven strokes. Each chime seemed to heighten her sense of foreboding. Something wasn't right. The air felt heavy, charged with an unseen presence that made the hairs on her arms stand on end.

Just as the clock in the hall struck midnight, a pounding at the door jolted Alice from her vigil. She raced through the darkened house, fumbling with the latch. When the door swung open, her heart plummeted.

Her father stood slumped against Mr Burton, a friend from the village. Reverend Wells was drenched to the bone, his face ashen in the dim light. Water dripped from his clothes, forming puddles on the threshold.

"Father!" Alice cried, reaching for him.

"I'm quite all right, my dear," he whispered, his voice barely audible. "Just a bit chilled. I tripped and fell into the river... Silly really... Just with the rain and wind and..."

But he was far from all right. As Alice helped Mr Burton guide her father inside, she noticed the laboured rise and fall of his chest, heard the rattle in his breath. His skin burned with fever despite his sodden clothes, and when he tried to stand unaided, his legs buckled beneath him.

ALONE

Alice scarcely left her father's side in the days that followed. She moved about the parsonage like a ghost, her footsteps quiet on the wooden floors as she carried steaming cups of willow bark tea and bowls of broth to his bedside. The doctor had come and gone, his expression grave as he'd packed away his instruments.

"Pneumonia," he'd murmured to Alice in the hallway, his voice low. "The river water has settled in his lungs. Keep him warm and comfortable."

The unspoken words hung between them. There was little else to be done.

Alice refused to accept this verdict. She piled blankets atop her father's trembling form, stoked the fire until sweat beaded on her own brow, and prayed with a desperation that made her voice crack. Each laboured breath her father took seemed to echo through the small bedroom, punctuated by coughing fits that left specks of blood on his handkerchief.

"You must rest, Father," she whispered, dabbing his forehead with a cool cloth.

His eyes, usually so bright and kind, had grown glassy with

fever. "I must finish... my sermon," he rasped, his fingers plucking weakly at the blankets. "The children... need an advocate."

On the third night, as rain continued to lash against the windows, Reverend Wells beckoned Alice to his bedside. His face had grown gaunt, the skin stretched taut over his cheekbones. Alice perched beside him, clutching her mother's Bible to her chest as tears welled in her eyes.

"My dearest child," he whispered, each word a struggle. "You have been... the greatest blessing."

"Please don't leave me," Alice pleaded, her voice small.

With tremendous effort, Reverend Wells lifted his hand and placed it atop the Bible she held. "This was your mother's greatest treasure," he said, his voice strengthening momentarily. "Now it is yours. Within these pages... you will find wisdom and comfort when I am gone."

His fingers tightened on the leather binding. "Write to Providence, dear heart, when I am gone. The Lord is ever listening."

Alice nodded, tears spilling down her cheeks.

"You have... her spirit," he murmured, his eyes drifting closed. "And my stubborn heart."

His hand fell away from the Bible, his breathing growing shallow. By morning, Reverend Stephen Wells had joined his beloved wife in heaven, leaving Alice feeling truly alone.

A BREWING STORM

Alice stood at the graveside, her mother's Bible clutched so tightly against her chest that its leather binding pressed painfully into her flesh. The pain felt right—a physical manifestation of the hollow ache inside her. Rain fell in a soft, persistent drizzle, as if the heavens themselves mourned Reverend Wells.

The entire village had gathered, mill workers standing alongside shopkeepers and farmers, their faces solemn beneath black umbrellas. Mrs Burton had dressed Alice in a borrowed black dress that hung loosely on her small frame. The woman's hand rested on Alice's shoulder, a steady presence in a world suddenly untethered.

"He was a good man," someone murmured behind her. "Too good for this world."

Alice watched as they lowered her father's coffin into the dark earth beside her mother's grave. The finality of it struck her with brutal force. She was truly alone now.

After the service, villagers crowded into the parsonage, bringing food and whispered condolences. Alice moved between them like a ghost, accepting embraces and kind words with numb politeness. Her mind kept returning to the letter she'd found in her father's desk—addressed to Mrs Margaret Pullman. Why would her father write to the wife of the man who had opposed him so vehemently? The question nagged at her even as she tried to focus on the present moment.

"Poor child," Mrs Wellings said to Mrs Burton in the kitchen, unaware that Alice stood just beyond the doorway. "Where will she go now?"

"That's for the church to decide, I suppose," Mrs Burton replied. "Though I hear there's a letter..."

Alice moved away, not wanting to hear what she already knew. Her future hung in the balance of that sealed envelope.

Near the window, she overheard Jack Finch's father speaking in hushed tones to another mill worker.

"Pullman knew exactly what he was doing, sending the Reverend out that night," he muttered darkly. "The man asked for him specifically, didn't he? On the worst night of flooding in years."

"Aye, and to the poorest part of town, where the water was highest," the other man agreed. "Retribution, plain as day, for those sermons about the children."

Alice froze, her heart pounding painfully against her ribs. Could it be true? Had Mr Pullman deliberately sent her father into danger, knowing he might fall ill? The thought made her dizzy with grief and anger.

Alice slipped away from the gathering downstairs, her legs carrying her mechanically up the narrow staircase to her small bedroom. The voices below faded to a distant murmur as she closed the door behind her. Rain pattered against the window, drawing her gaze outward to the churchyard where her father now lay beside her mother.

She sat on the edge of her bed, the mattress dipping beneath her slight weight. The borrowed black dress scratched against her skin, a constant reminder that nothing belonged to her anymore—not even her grief, which seemed to be communal property for the villagers to discuss and speculate upon.

"Write to Providence, dear heart, when I am gone," her father had said.

Alice opened the Bible, her mother's Bible, tracing the delicate handwriting that filled the margins. Notes on scripture, prayers, and observations about life and faith covered nearly every available space. This was her mother's voice, preserved in ink, and now her father's final gift.

From her small desk, Alice retrieved a worn journal and pencil. She hadn't the faintest notion how to address Providence —was it God? She thought so. She needed to pour out the storm inside her before it drowned her completely.

Dear Providence,

Father joined Mother in Heaven today. The rain hasn't stopped since they put him in the ground. I wonder if that's Your doing, or merely Yorkshire being Yorkshire. Father would say there's meaning in everything, even the weather.

They're all downstairs talking about what's to become of me. I heard Mr Finch say that Mr Pullman sent Father out deliberately that night, knowing the danger. Could a man truly be so cruel? Father always said to look for the good in everyone, but I find myself struggling to see any good in Mr Pullman.

I don't understand why You've taken both my parents. Father said suffering is one of faith's mysteries, but this mystery feels too heavy for me to carry. I'm afraid of what the letter to Mrs Pullman means.

Father believed in justice. He spoke truth even when it was dangerous. I don't know how to be brave like him, but I must try. If Mr Pullman truly caused Father's death, shouldn't someone speak that truth?

. . .

Alice looked up from the page, clutching the Bible to her chest as lightning flashed across the darkening sky. The storm was growing stronger, much like the resolve taking root in her heart.

PULLMAN MANOR

Alice stood in the empty parsonage, her mother's Bible clutched tightly to her chest. The musty scent of the room flooded her with conflicting memories. Sunlight streamed through the windows, illuminating dust motes that danced in the air, mocking the stillness that had settled over what was once a home filled with purpose and love.

She ran her fingers along the worn spines of her father's theological texts, arranged neatly on the bookshelf he had built himself. Each volume represented hours of discussion between them, lessons imparted not as father to child but as one soul to another. Now they belonged to the church, like everything else.

As Alice packed the few belongings she could carry—two dresses, her journal, a small wooden cross her father had carved—she felt a deep sense of dislocation. Every object she touched seemed to whisper memories: the chipped teacup from which her father drank each morning, the cushion her mother had embroidered before Alice was born. Her childhood haven was being abandoned as she prepared to face an uncertain future with the wife of the scariest man she knew, who had never before shown interest in her existence.

The carriage sent by the Pullman family arrived precisely at noon. Its driver, a stout man with ruddy cheeks, barely acknowledged Alice as he loaded her small trunk. He offered no words of comfort, no recognition of her grief—just cold indifference as Alice settled into the cramped space, her heart heavy with foreboding.

As the carriage clattered down the muddy roads, she gazed wistfully out of the window. The familiar landmarks of the village slipped past—the baker's shop where her father often stopped for fresh bread, the stream where they had collected wildflowers for her mother's grave. Alice clutched her mother's Bible, running her thumb over the worn leather binding. Her father's voice echoed in her memory: "Truth is light in darkness, Alice. Remember that always." Her heart ached at the loss of everything familiar.

The journey seemed both interminable and too brief. When the carriage finally rolled to a stop, Alice stared up at the imposing manor house with its towering walls and dark windows. Pullman Manor loomed against the grey sky like a fortress, its grandeur a stark contrast to the humble parsonage she had left behind. An overwhelming sense of dread washed over her as she stepped into the imposing foyer, her footsteps echoing on the marble floor.

Margaret Pullman descended the grand staircase, her silk dress rustling with each step. She greeted Alice with forced warmth, an uneasy smile painted across her face.

"Alice. Welcome to our home. Your father was my cousin, so that makes you... Well, family." The words sounded rehearsed, hollow. Behind her composure lay a tension that spoke of the family's complicated past with her father.

Alice curtseyed slightly, just as her father had taught her. "Thank you for receiving me, Mrs Pullman. My father asked me to give you this." She extended the sealed letter with trembling fingers.

Margaret took the letter, breaking the seal with a sharp nail. Her eyes moved across the page, and Alice watched as her expression shifted—first surprise, then something like regret, perhaps even guilt. She folded the letter carefully, tucking it into her sleeve.

"I see Stephen remembered our... connection." Margaret's voice softened momentarily, tinged with memories that Alice couldn't decipher.

Before Alice could respond, heavy footsteps announced another presence. Silas Pullman entered the foyer, his substantial frame casting a long shadow across the polished floor. He surveyed Alice with an appraising look, taking in her modest black dress and pale face.

"So this is the reverend's daughter." His voice boomed in the cavernous space. "How fortunate she has found a home with us."

Alice did not miss the excitement that glimmered in his dark eyes—not kindness or compassion, but calculation, as if he saw in her presence an opportunity to manipulate for his public image.

Alice followed Margaret and Silas deeper into the manor, her footsteps light against the polished floor. Each room they passed, displayed wealth beyond anything she had ever witnessed—ornate vases perched on marble pedestals, paintings in gilded frames, furniture with carved legs and velvet upholstery. The parsonage's simple comforts seemed a lifetime away.

Alice trailed behind Margaret, her small trunk already whisked away by a servant to some unknown corner of the house. The oppressive grandeur of Pullman Manor pressed in on her from all sides—ceilings that soared impossibly high, corridors that stretched into shadows. Each room they passed seemed designed to make one feel small and insignificant.

"This is the main drawing room," Margaret gestured without enthusiasm. "You'll not have cause to enter unless specifically invited."

Alice nodded, her throat too tight for words. She caught a glimpse of gleaming silver ornaments and furniture that looked too delicate to bear human weight.

As they turned a corner, a young woman appeared before them. She wore a dress of deep burgundy silk that rustled with her every movement. Her dark hair was arranged in an elaborate style that made her seem older than her years. She regarded Alice with open curiosity, her lips curling into something that wasn't quite a smile.

"Ah, Lavinia," Margaret said. "This is Alice Wells, Reverend Wells' daughter. She'll be staying with us now."

Lavinia Pullman's gaze swept over Alice's plain black dress and simple hair. "The charity case," she remarked, her voice sweet with poison. "How... quaint."

Alice felt heat rise to her cheeks but kept her eyes downcast, remembering her father's teachings about turning the other cheek. The memory brought a fresh wave of grief that threatened to overwhelm her.

"Lavinia," Silas cautioned, though without real conviction. There was a small glint in his eye.

"What? Everyone knows why she's here." Lavinia stepped closer, examining Alice as one might inspect damaged goods.

Alice looked up then, meeting Lavinia's eyes directly. She said nothing, but something in her steady gaze made Lavinia step back slightly.

"Well," Lavinia sniffed, "I suppose we must all make sacrifices for appearances. Do try to stay out of the way, won't you?" With that, she swept past them, the scent of expensive perfume lingering in her wake.

Margaret cleared her throat. "Come along, Alice."

"You'll take your meals in the kitchen," Margaret explained, not meeting Alice's eyes. "Mrs Reynolds will show you where everything is kept." Her voice carried a note of strained politeness that revealed the arrangement's true nature. This wasn't charity —it was penance.

"How fortunate that the church will see the Pullman family's generosity," Silas announced, as though speaking to an invisible audience rather than Alice. "Taking in the orphaned daughter of the late reverend—a man of good intentions, if somewhat misguided in his understanding of business matters."

Alice's throat tightened at the casual dismissal of her father's principles. She clutched her mother's Bible closer, drawing strength from its familiar weight.

"Your father's concerns for the mill children was admirable," Silas continued, his tone patronising, "though perhaps beyond the scope of his expertise. The church should focus on souls, not working conditions, wouldn't you agree?"

Before Alice could respond, Mr Grimsby appeared in the hallway, his grey eyes assessing her with cold calculation.

"Grimsby will show you to your quarters," Silas said. "We've prepared a suitable space for you."

Grimsby nodded curtly. "This way, girl."

Alice followed him up three flights of stairs, past the family bedrooms with their polished doors, through a narrow servants' passage, and finally up a steep, creaking staircase. The temperature dropped noticeably with each step.

"Here," Grimsby pushed open a door that groaned on its hinges.

The attic room stretched before her—bare walls, sloping ceiling, and a narrow iron bed pushed against the far wall. A small table with a chipped basin stood beneath a window that rattled against the wind. The floorboards were uneven and worn, with splinters that threatened to catch on stockings.

"Breakfast at six," Grimsby stated flatly. "Mrs Pullman expects you to earn your keep."

The door closed behind him with a decisive click. Alice stood alone in the cold room, shivering as she set her Bible on the windowsill. She sat on the bed, its thin mattress offering little comfort, and pulled the threadbare blanket around her shoulders.

From below, laughter drifted up—the sound of a young girl's voice, followed by the deeper tones of Silas. The sounds of family life continued without her, separated by floors and station and intention.

TWISTED CHAINS

The morning light filtered weakly through the attic window, casting long shadows across the uneven floorboards. Alice had barely slept, the unfamiliar creaks of Pullman Manor keeping her alert through the night. A sharp knock startled her fully awake.

"Up! Mrs Pullman expects you dressed and downstairs in ten minutes." The voice belonged to a housemaid Alice hadn't yet met.

Before Alice could respond, the door opened and a bundle of fabric landed on her bed.

"Miss Lavinia's old things. You're to wear these now."

Alice unfolded the bundle—a faded grey dress with frayed cuffs and a stain near the hem that hadn't quite washed out. The fabric felt rough against her fingers, nothing like her simple but well-cared-for clothes from the parsonage. She changed quickly, finding the dress hung awkwardly from her shoulders and cinched too tightly at the waist.

When she reached the bottom of the servants' staircase, Lavinia Pullman stood waiting, her own morning dress a vibrant blue that made Alice's hand-me-down look even more drab by comparison.

"Well, look at you," Lavinia circled Alice like a predator. "That dress never suited me, but on you—" She let out a theatrical sigh. "It's quite fitting for your station, I suppose."

Alice kept her eyes lowered, remembering her father's words about turning the other cheek. The dress scratched at her neck.

"When you pour the tea, try not to slop it everywhere," Lavinia continued. "Father can't abide uncouth manners at the breakfast table. Though I suppose parsonage life hardly prepared you for proper society."

The breakfast room fell silent as Alice entered. Silas looked up from his newspaper, his gaze sweeping over her ill-fitting attire with cold approval.

"Just in time for morning prayers," he announced. "Everyone will participate, of course."

Alice stood awkwardly at the edge of the family circle as Silas opened his leather-bound Bible with practiced ceremony. His voice filled the room with authority as he selected a passage from Ephesians.

"Children, obey your parents in the Lord, for this is right," he read, his eyes flicking briefly to Alice. "Honour thy father and mother, which is the first commandment with promise."

Each word seemed aimed directly at her, though he never looked up again. Alice felt the weight of expectation pressing down upon her shoulders.

"Servants, be obedient to them that are your masters according to the flesh, with fear and trembling, in singleness of your heart, as unto Christ," Silas continued, his voice rising with righteous fervour.

The words slipped under Alice's skin like splinters. This wasn't the loving God her father had taught her about—this was scripture twisted into chains.

STRENGTHEN THINE HEART

The weeks passed in a blur of endless chores and cold silences. Alice's hands grew raw from scrubbing floors, polishing silver, and mending Lavinia's garments. Each night, she climbed the narrow servants' staircase to her attic room, her body aching with exhaustion, her heart heavy with loneliness.

In the quiet darkness, Alice would trace her fingers over the worn leather cover of her mother's Bible, remembering how her father's voice had made the passages come alive with warmth and wisdom. The Pullmans' morning prayers twisted scripture into something unrecognisable—cold commandments of obedience rather than messages of love and justice.

"I miss you, Father," she whispered into the stillness one night. "I miss our talks about Providence and purpose."

She pulled out the small notebook she'd hidden beneath her thin mattress and began to write by the faint moonlight streaming through her window.

Dear Providence,

The manor feels colder each day, though summer approaches. Not in temperature, but in spirit. Mr Pullman speaks of God as if He were a stern taskmaster, not the loving shepherd Father taught me about. I wonder if they worship the same deity at all.

Sometimes I hear Father's voice so clearly in my mind that I turn, expecting to see him. The disappointment cuts fresh each time.

On Wednesday afternoon, Alice was polishing the ornate mirror in the grand salon when Lavinia swept in with three elegantly dressed young women. Alice tried to make herself invisible, focusing intently on her work.

"Oh, don't mind her," Lavinia's voice carried across the room. "That's the charity case—the dead reverend's daughter. Father took her in for appearances' sake, though Mother was against it. Apparently, we're cousins, though you'd never guess it to look at her."

The young women tittered behind gloved hands.

"Does she actually believe she's one of the family?" one asked.

"Heavens, no!" Lavinia laughed. "Though I caught her staring at my music books the other day. As if a girl like that could ever learn to play properly."

Alice's cheeks burned. The polishing cloth trembled in her hand as tears threatened to spill. She thought of her father's gentle voice: *"True dignity, Alice, comes not from how others treat you, but from how you respond to that treatment."*

Taking a deep breath, Alice continued her work, her movements deliberate and careful. She would not give Lavinia the satisfaction of seeing her crumble.

That night, Alice knelt beside her bed, the floorboards hard against her knees. She clutched her mother's Bible to her chest.

. . .

"Dear Providence," she whispered, *"grant me the strength to be kind when they are cruel, to be honest when they deceive, and to remember who I truly am when they try to make me forget. I am Alice Wells, daughter of Reverend Stephen Wells, and though I may serve in this house, my spirit remains my own."*

She opened the Bible to Psalm 27, running her finger along the verse her father had underlined: *"Wait on the Lord: be of good courage, and he shall strengthen thine heart."*

~

Alice tried to keep her head down during the Pullman family's mealtimes. She'd learned that being invisible was her best defence, though Edgar Pullman — Lavinia's younger brother — seemed determined to make that impossible.

"Look at her hunched over like that," Edgar said one evening as Alice cleared the dinner plates. At thirteen, he was caught between boyhood and the man he would become, his voice occasionally cracking mid-sentence. "Do they not teach posture at parsonages?"

Lavinia's tinkling laugh followed. "Perhaps she's searching for crumbs. Father's charity only extends so far, after all."

Alice's hands trembled slightly as she stacked the fine china, careful not to chip the gold-rimmed edges.

"I think she's looking for somewhere to hide that dreadful hair," Edgar continued, emboldened by his sister's approval. "It's the colour of dishwater."

Alice felt her cheeks burn but kept her eyes fixed on her task. She thought of her father's gentle hands braiding her hair on Sunday mornings, telling her it reminded him of chestnuts in autumn. The memory strengthened her resolve not to let them see her pain.

"Perhaps we should cut it off while she sleeps," Lavinia

suggested, her voice light but her eyes cold. "It would be an improvement, don't you think, Edgar?"

Edgar hesitated, something flickering across his face before he nodded. "Certainly couldn't make her look any worse."

As Alice carried the stack of plates toward the kitchen, Edgar deliberately stretched his leg into her path. She stumbled but managed to steady herself before the dishes could crash to the floor.

"Clumsy as well as plain," he observed to his sister's delight.

That night, Alice sat on her thin mattress, clutching her mother's Bible to her chest. The moonlight cast long shadows across the attic floor as she listened to the distant sounds of music from the drawing room below. The Pullmans were entertaining guests, their laughter occasionally rising through the floorboards like bubbles in a pond.

She opened her journal, dipped her pen in the small inkpot she'd salvaged from her father's desk, and began to write.

Dear Providence,

I wonder if You see them—Edgar and Lavinia—not as they appear to me, but as they truly are. Father would say there must be goodness in everyone, but I confess I struggle to find it in them.

ALLIES

Alice stood in the kitchen that evening, watching Cook prepare dinner for the family. Her own stomach grumbled as she eyed the roast beef, potatoes, and fresh vegetables being arranged on fine china. The day had been particularly harsh—Lavinia had found fault with Alice's dusting of the library and made her redo every shelf twice. Alice's arms ached from the repetitive motion, and her back throbbed from bending to scrub the entrance hall floor afterward.

When Cook slid a plate toward her with a thin slice of bread and a meagre portion of yesterday's stew, Alice tried not to show her disappointment. The portions had grown smaller over the weeks, as if someone had instructed the staff to provide her with just enough to survive but never enough to satisfy.

Mrs Reynolds, the housekeeper, paused by the kitchen table. Her keen eyes took in Alice's forlorn expression as the girl stared at her inadequate meal.

"Cook," Mrs Reynolds called, "I need to check the pantry inventory. Alice, come help me with the counting, would you?"

Once in the pantry, Mrs Reynolds pulled a cloth-wrapped

bundle from her apron pocket and pressed it into Alice's hands. "Quickly now," she whispered.

Inside was a thick slice of bread still warm from the oven, spread with butter and a dab of honey. Alice's eyes widened.

"Eat it before you go back," Mrs Reynolds said, her voice low but kind. "Don't let them break you, child. Your father was a good man who spoke truth to the powerful. That's something they fear, not something to be ashamed of."

"Thank you," Alice whispered, the simple kindness bringing unexpected tears to her eyes.

"We must be clever about it," Mrs Reynolds continued, watching the door. "But you're not alone in this house, remember that."

Over the following weeks, Alice discovered small mercies hidden throughout her days. A warm currant muffin appeared in her apron pocket while she hung laundry. A cup of sweet tea materialised beside her when she polished silver late into the evening. Each gift came with Mrs Reynolds' knowing glance—a quiet conspiracy of kindness in a house that offered little.

One afternoon, as Alice scrubbed the drawing room windows under Lavinia's critical gaze, Mrs Reynolds appeared in the doorway.

"Miss Lavinia, pardon the interruption. Alice, I need your assistance in the pantry immediately. The preserves need reorganising before your mother's tea guests arrive tomorrow."

In the safety of the pantry, Alice's shoulders relaxed for the first time that day.

"That girl," Mrs Reynolds muttered, arranging jars on a shelf. "Takes after her father in all the wrong ways. The Pullmans weren't always like this, you know. Mrs Pullman—Margaret—she and your father were quite close as children. Cousins, of course, but more like siblings then."

Alice stared at Mrs Reynolds, her hands stilling on the preserves jar she'd been holding. "Mrs Pullman and my father were close?" The idea seemed impossible given the cold distance Margaret maintained whenever Alice entered a room.

"Oh yes," Mrs Reynolds nodded, reaching past Alice to straighten a row of pickled vegetables. "Thick as thieves as children, so I've heard. Apparently, your grandmother—her aunt—would have them both stay during summers. Before she married Mr Pullman, Miss Margaret had quite a different light in her eyes."

Alice absorbed this revelation, trying to reconcile it with the withdrawn woman who barely acknowledged her presence. "What happened between them?"

Mrs Reynolds glanced toward the pantry door before lowering her voice. "She chose wealth, some might say. Mr Pullman is a very wealthy man, and would keep Margaret finically secure. There were... expectations. Family pressures." She sighed. "Your father chose the church, she chose security. Different paths that couldn't cross again."

Alice thought of her father's compassion, how he found goodness in everyone. Had he maintained that same grace toward his cousin who'd turned away from him?

"The letter," Alice whispered. "Father sent her a letter with me."

Mrs Reynolds nodded but said no more as footsteps approached the pantry. She quickly pressed a small apple into Alice's apron pocket. "Best get back to your windows before Miss Lavinia comes looking."

That night, lying on her thin mattress, Alice held her mother's Bible close. The connection between her father and Mrs Pullman felt like a missing piece of a puzzle she hadn't known existed. What had been in that letter? And if they'd once been close, why did Margaret allow her to be treated so poorly now?

Alice opened her journal.

. . .

Perhaps there are remnants of kindness in unexpected places, she wrote. *Mrs Reynolds risks much to show me small mercies. And Mrs Pullman—who knows what memories my presence stirs in her? Father always said to look for the light, even in the darkest corners.*

Alice completed her morning chores with particular haste. The household still slept, offering her a rare moment of solitude. She slipped outside, drawn to the misty gardens where droplets clung to every leaf and petal like tiny glass beads.

The soft earth yielded beneath her worn shoes as she wandered between neatly trimmed hedgerows. The scent of damp soil and early roses filled her lungs—a welcome change from the stuffy confines of the manor. As she rounded a corner, Alice spotted an elderly man kneeling beside a flowerbed, his weathered hands gently working the soil.

"Good morning, miss," he called, his voice warm and cracked with age. "You must be Reverend Wells' daughter."

Alice paused, surprised at the kindness in his tone. "Yes, sir. I'm Alice."

The old gardener's eyes crinkled as he smiled. "Thomas Buckley, at your service. I've been tending these gardens since before you were born." He studied her face with gentle curiosity. "My word, you look just like her."

"Like who?" Alice stepped closer.

Alice's heart quickened. "You knew my mother?"

"Indeed I did. She grew up in the village. She had a gift with growing things." Thomas pointed to a cluster of white roses. "Those were her favourites. She'd say they reminded her of stars fallen to earth."

Alice knelt beside him, suddenly desperate to hear more. "Please, tell me about her."

"She laughed like summer rain—gentle but filling everything

around her." Thomas demonstrated the delicate way Eleanor would cup blossoms in her palm. "Always asking questions about every plant. Not just their names, but their stories—where they came from, how they survived winter, what they needed to thrive."

Each detail was precious to Alice, who had so few memories of her own. She found herself returning whenever possible, slipping away between chores to seek Thomas in the garden. He taught her how certain flowers closed before storms, how roots grew stronger when faced with resistance.

"See these peonies?" he said one morning. "They need the cold of winter to bloom properly in spring. Without that hardship, they'd never show their beauty."

On her fourth visit, Thomas pressed a small paper packet into her palm. "Forget-me-not seeds," he whispered. "Your mother planted these everywhere. They're stubborn little things—grow in the most unlikely places."

Alice clutched the packet, this tangible connection to her mother making her throat tighten.

"Plant them somewhere secret," Thomas advised. "Watch them grow. They'll remind you of the love that's always with you, no matter how hard things seem."

CLOSE TO HOPE

Alice froze in the hallway, hands trembling as she clutched the stack of freshly laundered linens. Lavinia's shrill voice carried from the drawing room, where she entertained two friends from the village.

"You should see her—the charity case—shuffling about like some wounded animal. Father insists we keep her, says it shows Christian charity." Lavinia's laughter cut through Alice like a knife. "As if anyone believes that. She wears my old dresses like a scarecrow."

"How dreadful for you," one of the visitors sympathised.

"Truly," Lavinia laughed.

Alice bit her lip hard enough to taste blood.

"That's not fair."

The quiet voice startled Alice. Edgar stood at the end of the corridor, his face flushed with what appeared to be embarrassment.

"What did you say?" Lavinia's tone sharpened.

"I said it's not fair how you speak of her." Edgar's voice gained strength. "She's lost everything, Lavinia. Her home, her father—everything."

Alice pressed herself against the wall, hardly daring to breathe.

"Don't be ridiculous, Edgar. She's fortunate to have a roof over her head at all."

"Is she? When you mock her constantly? When she eats alone in the kitchen?" Edgar shook his head. "Father may speak of Christian charity, but I've seen precious little of it shown to her."

Alice held her breath, hardly daring to move as she listened to the exchange between Edgar and Lavinia. The stack of linens trembled in her arms, her knuckles white with tension.

"You're being absurd, Edgar," Lavinia's voice turned venomous. "Just last week you were laughing about her thread-bare stockings. And didn't you trip her in the dining room? Don't pretend to be saintly now."

Alice's cheeks burned at the reminder of these humiliations. She pressed closer to the wall, wishing she could disappear into it entirely.

"That was different," Edgar mumbled, his voice losing some of its conviction.

"Different how?" Lavinia pressed, her tone triumphant. "You've been just as cruel as I have."

A heavy silence followed. Alice waited, her heart hammering against her ribs. She knew she should walk away, continue with her chores, but her feet refused to move.

"I thought..." Edgar's voice dropped lower, forcing Alice to strain to hear him. "I thought it was just a game at first. I didn't think about how it felt for her."

Lavinia scoffed. "Oh, spare me—"

"No, listen," Edgar interrupted, his voice growing firmer. "It doesn't feel fun anymore. Not when I see her face afterward. Not when I think about what Father Wells would say if he knew how we treated his daughter."

Alice nearly gasped aloud at the mention of her father. No one in this house ever spoke his name.

"Father Wells?" Lavinia's voice dripped with contempt. "The man who criticised our father's business from his pulpit? Who are you to—"

"He was kind to me once," Edgar said quietly. "When I was ill last winter and he visited. He spoke to me like I mattered, not just as Silas Pullman's son."

Alice felt tears prick her eyes. That sounded exactly like her father—seeing the person beneath the name, the wealth, the circumstance.

"You're becoming pathetic," Lavinia snapped. "Next you'll be reading scripture with the charity case."

Footsteps approached, and Alice hurried away before she could be discovered eavesdropping. Her mind whirled with confusion. Edgar, defending her? The same boy who had tripped her only weeks before?

The next morning at breakfast, Alice silently collected the empty plates. The family had finished eating, but Edgar lingered, fidgeting with something beneath the table.

"Alice," he called softly as she reached the door. He approached, glancing over his shoulder to ensure they were alone. "I thought you might enjoy this." He extended a small leather-bound book. "It's Robinson Crusoe. About a man who survives alone on an island. I—I just thought you might like it."

Alice stared at the book, then at Edgar's uncertain expression.

"Thank you," she whispered, tucking it carefully into her apron pocket. "But why—"

"I know what it's like to feel alone, even in a house full of people." His eyes met hers briefly before darting away. "Perhaps we could talk about it when you've read some? I'd like to know your thoughts."

For the first time since arriving at Pullman Manor, Alice felt a small flicker of warmth in her chest—not quite hope, but something close to it.

DEAR PROVIDENCE

Alice climbed the narrow attic stairs, each step heavier than the last. She had gotten used to the ache in her shoulders by now. Through the small dormer window, the last golden rays of sunset painted the eaves, casting long shadows across her sparse room. The manor had fallen quiet save for distant voices downstairs—the Pullmans entertaining guests again, their laughter floating up like a foreign language she could no longer translate.

She waited, listening for footsteps on the stairs, for Mrs Reynolds making her final rounds. When only silence greeted her, Alice knelt beside her bed and pried at the floorboard that had caught her attention during her first week. It lifted with a soft creak, revealing the small hollowed out space beneath. From this secret space, she withdrew her most precious possessions: a journal bound in faded blue cloth and a small inkpot she'd salvaged from her father's study before leaving the parsonage.

The journal's blank pages seemed to breathe as she opened it, the crisp scent of paper rising to meet her. Alice ran her fingers across the paper's surface, feeling an unexpected calm settle over her. Here, at least, was a place that belonged solely to her—a place where Lavinia's mockery and Silas's condescension couldn't reach.

Dipping her pen into the ink, she hesitated only briefly before writing at the top of the latest page: The words flowed more easily after that, as though a dam had broken inside her:

Dear Providence,

I wonder if Father was right about You always listening. I find myself hoping so, for I've never felt more alone than since he joined Mother in Heaven. The parsonage stands empty now, and I with it—a hollow shell where warmth once lived. Father would say that's dramatic, but he would smile when he said it, his eyes crinkling at the corners.

Alice paused, blinking back tears before continuing:

I miss our conversations most. The way Father would consider my questions about scripture as though they mattered. The gentle corrections when I misunderstood. The pride in his voice when I grasped something difficult. Here, no one speaks to me except to issue commands or criticisms. Mr. Pullman's morning prayers feel nothing like Father's—they are performances meant to demonstrate his piety rather than conversations with God.

Her pen scratched steadily across the page, the sound oddly comforting in the silence:

. . .

Lavinia called me 'scarecrow' again today, and her friends laughed. I wanted to remind her that Father taught me pride comes before a fall, but then I realized I was feeling pride myself—wounded pride. Is that sinful, Providence? To wish to defend oneself against cruelty? Father would say we must turn the other cheek, but I wonder if he truly understood how difficult that becomes when both cheeks are already stinging.

Alice's pen hovered over the page for a moment before she continued writing.

Today marks one year since Father joined Mother in Heaven. Mr. Pullman spoke harshly of Father during dinner, calling his concern for the mill children 'misguided sentimentality.' Father taught me that You are a God of truth, even when truth brings discomfort...

Her hand trembled slightly, but she pressed on, the words flowing from some deep well within her.

I wonder sometimes if I'm meant to forget Father's teachings now that I live under this roof. Mr Pullman's God seems so different—a God who favours the wealthy and turns blind eyes to suffering. But I cannot believe that. The God Father showed me sees the sparrow fall, counts the hairs on our heads, and surely counts the tears of children working twelve hours at the looms.

Alice paused, listening to the distant sounds of the household below. The scratch of her pen against paper felt like a small rebellion.

. . .

I am confused, Providence. Why was Father taken when his work seemed unfinished? Why must I live with those who dishonour his memory? Yet even in my confusion, I feel Your presence. When Thomas shows me how the garden grows, when Mrs Reynolds slips an extra piece of bread onto my plate, when Edgar offers a moment of kindness—these small mercies remind me You haven't abandoned me.

Each evening, Alice returned to her journal, kneeling beside the loose floorboard as though at an altar. The ritual brought her father closer somehow. She could almost hear his voice as she wrote of her daily struggles and small victories.

Father once told me that faith isn't the absence of doubt but the courage to seek truth despite it. When he spoke against the conditions at the mill, he wasn't being sentimental—he was being faithful. "Alice," he would say, "we must not confuse comfort with righteousness." I carry these words with me when Mr Pullman's prayers ring hollow.

What had begun as letters to an unseen Providence gradually transformed into something more—a conversation with herself, a mapping of her heart's journey. Alice found herself writing not just of sorrows but of hope.

I dream sometimes of teaching children to read as Father taught me. Of helping those who cannot help themselves. Perhaps one day I might even speak truth to powerful, wealthy people as Father did. Is that too bold a dream for a girl with nothing?

. . .

In these quiet moments, the manor's oppressive atmosphere receded. Lavinia's cutting remarks and Silas's thunderous pronouncements faded to insignificance. Alice's attic room, once a prison, became a sanctuary where her true self could breathe.

Re-reading her entries from months past, Alice traced her finger over the words. They reflected not just her pain but her growth—a testament to survival. She hugged the journal to her chest, feeling its weight against her heart.

I will not forget who I am, Providence. I am Reverend Wells's daughter. I will stand for truth and justice, even when it brings discomfort. I will trust that You are listening, guiding my steps, even when the path seems dark. Father would expect nothing less.

WILLIAM THORNTON

William Thornton adjusted his collar as he approached the wrought-iron gates of Pullman Manor. The morning air carried a crisp bite that reddened his cheeks and made his breath visible in small, dissipating clouds. Sunlight glinted off the imposing stone façade, illuminating the manor's grandeur while casting long shadows across the manicured lawn. William paused, taking in the sight before him—three stories of Yorkshire limestone, tall windows reflecting the morning light, chimneys standing like sentinels against the clear blue sky.

"Right then," he muttered to himself, squaring his shoulders. "First impressions and all that."

The leather satchel hung heavy at his side, filled with carefully selected texts on Latin, mathematics, and natural philosophy. His fingers brushed the worn spine of Plato's Republic—a personal favourite he hoped might spark intellectual curiosity in young Edgar Pullman. Cambridge had filled William's head with progressive notions about education, ideas that challenged the rigid rote learning so common in households like this. Children needed encouragement to question, not merely recite.

"Education ought to be a dialogue, not a monologue," his favourite professor had often said.

The gravel crunched beneath his boots as he approached the entrance. A stern-faced butler opened the door before William could knock, eyeing him with thinly veiled suspicion.

"Mr Thornton, I presume. Mr Pullman is expecting you in his study."

The entrance hall swallowed William in cold grandeur. Marble floors echoed his footsteps, multiplying them until it seemed a small army marched through the house. How different from Cambridge's warm wooden corridors where ideas flowed as freely as ale at the college feasts.

The butler rapped sharply on a heavy oak door, then stepped aside.

"The new tutor, sir."

Silas Pullman sat behind an enormous desk, his substantial frame dwarfing the furniture. He didn't rise when William entered, merely assessed him with calculating eyes that seemed to measure William's worth in pounds and shillings.

"Thornton. Cambridge, was it?"

"Yes, sir. First in my year in Classics."

"Hmm." Pullman's gaze flicked over William's modest attire. "Academic achievement is all well and good, but I require practical results. My son requires preparation for his future responsibilities. No filling his head with radical nonsense."

"I assure you, sir, my methods are thorough and effective."

"They'd better be. Edgar will inherit considerable interests one day."

William felt the weight of unspoken expectations pressing down upon him. The room itself seemed to close in—dark wood panelling, heavy curtains, and the persistent ticking of a grandfather clock marking each second of this uncomfortable exchange.

"You'll begin with Edgar this afternoon. Mr Grimsby, my

assistant, will show you to the library where you'll conduct your lessons."

William nodded, clutching his satchel tighter. Somewhere in this imposing house was a fourteen-year-old boy whose mind he would help shape. Despite the chill in the air, William felt a spark of purpose ignite within him. Perhaps here, in this most unlikely of places, he might make a genuine difference.

William followed Mr Grimsby, his mind still replaying the conversation with Mr Pullman. The cold, calculated nature of the man's expectations weighed on him. So focused was he on these thoughts that he nearly stumbled over a figure kneeling on the marble floor.

A young woman scrubbed vigorously at the tiles. Her thin arms worked the brush in circular motions, her knuckles red and raw from the harsh soap. Chestnut hair escaped from beneath a simple cap, framing a face that, despite its pallor, possessed a quiet dignity. Her brown dress, patched and worn at the edges, hung loosely on her slender frame.

William paused, watching her struggle with a heavy wooden bucket as she attempted to move it across the floor. Water sloshed dangerously close to the rim with each effort. Without thinking, he stepped forward.

"Let me help you with that."

His hand closed over hers on the bucket handle. The touch lasted only a moment, but William felt a jolt of awareness at the contact—her skin was cold yet somehow ignited a warmth within him. Their eyes met, and William found himself looking into the deepest brown eyes he'd ever seen, filled with surprise and something else—a resilience that belied her fragile appearance.

Those eyes held wisdom beyond her years, a quiet strength that made William's breath catch. Despite her humble position, she carried herself with grace that spoke of better circumstances once known. The girl seemed startled by his kindness, as though such simple human decency had become foreign to her.

"Thank you, sir," she whispered, her voice soft yet clear.

Before William could respond, the sharp click of heels against marble cut through the moment. A young woman in an elaborate gown of emerald silk approached, her face twisting with disdain.

"Mr Thornton, I presume?" Her tone dripped with affected superiority. "I see you've met our little charity case. Do leave her be—the work builds character in those lacking proper breeding."

The girl immediately withdrew her hand from the bucket, her eyes downcast, a flush of humiliation staining her cheeks. William felt a surge of indignation at the casual cruelty.

"Miss Pullman," he acknowledged with a stiff bow, recognising Lavinia from description. "I was merely offering assistance."

"How quaint," Lavinia replied with a dismissive wave. "But unnecessary. Alice knows her place."

William straightened, meeting Lavinia's gaze with steady determination. In that moment, he made a silent promise to himself—this household would not define his approach to education or human dignity. He would create a sanctuary of learning for young Edgar, regardless of the family's attitudes.

And the girl—Alice—he would remember her. There was something in her quiet resilience that spoke to him, a strength that deserved recognition rather than scorn. Though he had no idea how, William knew he could not simply ignore the injustice of her situation.

A NEW PERSPECTIVE

William arranged his books on the small desk in the library, taking a moment to appreciate the collection surrounding him. Though not extensive as Cambridge's libraries, the shelves held respectable volumes—mostly unread, judging by their pristine spines. The room smelled of leather and beeswax polish, its heavy curtains casting the space in perpetual twilight despite the afternoon sun outside.

The door swung open with unnecessary force as Edgar Pullman sauntered in. The boy's resemblance to his father was striking—the same square jaw and dark eyes, though lacking the hardness years of business dealings had etched into the elder Pullman's face.

"Father says you're to teach me Latin and mathematics," Edgar announced, dropping into a chair without waiting for instruction. "Though I don't see much point in dead languages."

William noted the challenging tone, the tilt of chin that suggested the boy was repeating opinions he'd heard rather than formed himself.

"Latin isn't merely a dead language, Edgar. It's the foundation of scientific naming, legal terminology, and philosophical thought that shapes our modern world." William pulled out a volume of Cicero. "Even your father's business contracts likely contain Latin phrases."

Edgar shrugged. "Lavinia says tutors are just failed scholars who couldn't make their own way."

The words stung, but William recognised them as Lavinia's barbs rather than Edgar's. He changed tack.

"Tell me, what interests you, Edgar? What makes you curious about the world?"

The question seemed to catch the boy off guard. He shifted in his seat.

"Father says I'm to learn what's practical for running the mill one day."

William nodded thoughtfully. "And what do you think makes a good mill owner?"

Edgar's brow furrowed. "Making profit, I suppose."

"Is that all?" William leaned forward. "What of the people who work for you? Don't their lives factor into good business?"

"They're paid wages," Edgar replied, but uncertainty crept into his voice.

"Let's approach this differently." William closed the Latin text. "If you owned the mill tomorrow, what would you change?"

Edgar's eyes widened at this unexpected question. For the first time, genuine interest flickered across his features.

"The machines," he said after a moment. "They're dangerous. Timothy—one of the workers' sons—lost two fingers last month."

William nodded encouragingly. "That's precisely the kind of thinking that separates a mere businessman from a true leader. Progress isn't measured solely in pounds and shillings."

William watched Edgar's expression change, the façade of disinterest crumbling as he spoke about the mill accidents.

There was something genuine there—concern that hadn't been entirely stamped out by his father's influence.

"I've heard workers talking," Edgar continued, his voice dropping as though sharing a secret. "They say the machines could be made safer with proper guards, but Father says the modifications cost too much."

William nodded, careful not to betray his own opinions too forcefully. "Mathematics has practical applications beyond counting profits. Engineering calculations could determine how to make those machines safer while maintaining efficiency."

Edgar straightened in his chair. "I hadn't thought of it that way."

"That's what education offers—new ways of seeing familiar problems." William tapped the desk. "Latin may seem useless, but it teaches precision of thought. Every successful modification to those machines will require precise thinking."

The library door creaked, and William glanced up to see Alice slipping in with a feather duster. She kept her eyes downcast, moving quietly toward the far shelves.

Edgar followed William's gaze, his posture stiffening. The boy seemed suddenly uncomfortable, casting furtive glances between William and Alice.

"Shall we begin with Euclid?" William asked, deliberately shifting attention back to their lesson.

As they worked through geometric principles, William noticed Edgar's occasional glances toward Alice as she methodically dusted the shelves. There was something in those looks—not the contempt he'd witnessed in Lavinia, but something more complex. Guilt, perhaps?

When their lesson concluded, Edgar gathered his books with unusual care. "Same time tomorrow, Mr Thornton?"

"Indeed. Please review the first three propositions."

As Edgar reached the door, he paused. "Alice," he called, his voice awkward but not unkind, "I left that book we discussed on the side table."

She looked up, surprise evident in her quick glance. "Thank you, Master Edgar."

After the boy left, William noticed a worn copy of Middlemarch where Edgar had indicated. Interesting, he thought. Perhaps there was more to young Master Pullman than initially met the eye.

Alice climbed the narrow staircase to her attic room. The wooden boards creaked beneath her worn shoes, announcing her retreat to the only space that felt remotely her own. The chill of evening had already settled into the small chamber, seeping through the thin walls and single window where moonlight now spilled across the floorboards.

She closed the door behind her and leaned against it, exhaling a breath she hadn't realised she'd been holding. For a moment, she stood perfectly still, listening to the distant sounds of the household below—Lavinia's high-pitched laughter, the clink of glasses, the muffled conversation that would continue for hours without her.

Alice knelt beside her bed and reached for the loose floorboard, her fingers finding the familiar groove. She lifted it carefully, retrieving her journal and mother's Bible from their hiding place. The leather binding felt warm against her palms, as though it carried some remnant of her father's touch.

She settled onto her thin mattress, wrapping the threadbare blanket around her shoulders against the evening chill. The candle beside her bed cast dancing shadows across the page as she opened her journal.

. . .

Dear Providence,

Today I met someone who looked at me as though I were visible. I've found out that his name is William Thornton, the new tutor. He offered to help me with my bucket—such a small kindness that nearly brought tears to my eyes. How strange that after months of disappearing into the walls of this house, a simple acknowledgement of my struggle should affect me so deeply.

Alice paused, her pen hovering above the page. She recalled the warmth in William's eyes, so unlike the cold calculation in Mr. Pullman's gaze or the casual cruelty in Lavinia's.

He has kind eyes—the sort Father would have called "windows to a thoughtful soul." When Lavinia interrupted us, calling me "the charity case," I saw something in his expression. Not pity, which I've grown to despise, but recognition. As though he understood something about me that even I have forgotten.

Edgar seems different around him as well. Perhaps Mr Thornton's presence awakens conscience, like sunlight touching frozen ground.

Alice dipped her pen again, the scratching against paper the only sound in her small room.

I wonder if this is what hope feels like—this fragile thing taking root despite the barren soil. Father always said truth and kindness find each other eventually. Perhaps in this cold house, there might yet be unexpected allies.

I must be careful not to build castles from mere pebbles. But tonight, I feel less alone.

CLANDESTINE CORRESPONDENCE

Alice methodically dusted the shelves of the Pullman Manor library. Sunlight streamed through the tall windows, illuminating dust motes that danced in the air like tiny messengers. The room's towering bookshelves surrounded her with a comforting embrace of aged paper and leather bindings, so different from the cold indifference that permeated the rest of the house.

She moved with practiced efficiency, yet her attention kept wandering to the spines of theological texts that reminded her so powerfully of her father's study. Her fingers brushed against a familiar volume—Augustine's Confessions in Latin. Alice paused, drawn to the text despite herself. She opened the book carefully, her eyes falling upon a passage she remembered her father translating.

"Fecisti nos ad te et inquietum est cor nostrum donec requiescat in te," she mouthed silently, her heart swelling with a sense of connection to her father's teachings. "Thou hast made us for thyself, O Lord, and our heart is restless until it finds its rest in thee."

Lost in her world of literature, Alice didn't notice William's entrance. He stood quietly in the doorway, watching as her lips moved silently in rhythm with the words. The morning light caught the chestnut highlights in her hair, revealing an expression of such earnest concentration that he found himself reluctant to interrupt.

William observed her expressive face as she turned a page, noting how her brow furrowed slightly at a challenging passage before smoothing in understanding. There was a depth of insight and intelligence in her countenance that reflected her father's legacy—a stark contrast to the disdainful treatment dictated by her position in the Pullman household.

Stepping forward, his footfall deliberately audible on the wooden floor, William addressed her directly. "Alice, may I ask what you're reading?"

His use of her name caught her off guard. Not "girl" or "you there" or "the charity case," but "Alice"—as though she were a person worthy of recognition. The book nearly slipped from her fingers as she looked up, startled.

Their eyes met across the sunlit space. Alice felt her heart racing, not from fear but from a sense of recognition that transcended their class differences. There was genuine interest in his gaze, not the dismissive glance she'd grown accustomed to.

"Augustine, sir," she answered, her voice barely above a whisper. "His Confessions."

"You understand Latin?" William approached, his tone curious rather than accusatory.

"Some," Alice admitted, emboldened by his approachability. "My father taught me the basics. This passage speaks of how our hearts remain restless until they find rest in God."

"Remarkable interpretation." William's eyes widened slightly. "Most tutors struggle to convey that nuance to university students."

"The words themselves are beautiful," Alice ventured, "but

I've often wondered if restlessness might also be God's gift—pushing us toward greater understanding."

William considered this, his head tilting thoughtfully. "An insightful perspective. Augustine might agree that divine discontent spurs spiritual growth." He studied her with newfound appreciation. "Your father taught you well."

Alice's heart raced as she carefully placed Augustine's Confessions back on the shelf. William's recognition of her intellect lingered in her mind long after he'd left the library. She ran her fingers along the spines of the books, a small smile playing at her lips.

Three days later, while dusting the far corner shelves, Alice noticed something peculiar. A slim volume of poetry had been placed spine-inward, contrary to the meticulous organisation of the rest of the library. Curious, she pulled it out to correct its placement when a folded piece of paper slipped from between its pages.

The handwriting was neat and measured: *Matthew 10:31 - 'Fear ye not therefore, ye are of more value than many sparrows.' Your insights on Augustine was remarkable. You might find Blake's perspective on divine vision of interest. -W*

Alice's hands trembled as she clutched the note. Someone had seen her—truly seen her—for the first time since Father died.

Over the following weeks, more books appeared in unlikely places: Wordsworth's poetry, Mary Wollstonecraft's writings, and theological texts she'd never encountered before. Each contained notes in William's hand, sometimes challenging her with questions about the text, other times offering biblical passages that spoke of human dignity and worth.

Consider Isaiah 43:1 - 'Fear not: for I have redeemed thee, I have called thee by thy name; thou art mine.' Your thoughts on Wordsworth's connection between nature and divine presence reminded me of this passage.

These discoveries became the brightest moments in Alice's otherwise dreary existence. She began to anticipate her library duties with quiet excitement rather than resignation. While the Pullmans spoke over her as though she were invisible, William's notes acknowledged her mind, her spirit, her very personhood.

One afternoon, after ensuring she was alone, Alice daringly penned her own response on a scrap of paper torn from her journal: *Psalm 139:14 - 'I will praise thee; for I am fearfully and wonderfully made.' Blake's visions remind me that seeing beyond the material world requires faith and imagination. Both gifts from Providence. -A*

She slipped it into Milton's Paradise Lost, which William had mentioned in his previous note, and placed the book at an angle that would catch his attention.

Thus began their clandestine correspondence. Through carefully selected verses and literary reflections, Alice and William developed a dialogue that nourished her starving soul. Though their face-to-face interactions remained brief and formal under the watchful eyes of the household, their written exchanges created a sanctuary of mutual understanding.

TRULY SEEN

Alice's fingers traced the edge of the worn journal as she entered the library, clutching it closer to her chest when she heard footsteps approaching. The familiar rhythm of William's gait brought a warmth to her cheeks that she couldn't quite suppress. In recent weeks, their literary correspondence had evolved from cautious exchanges to something deeper—a meeting of minds that increasingly felt like a lifeline in her isolated existence.

"You've brought your journal today," William observed quietly, ensuring no one else was within earshot.

Alice nodded, her eyes bright with purpose. "I've been contemplating the passage from Amos you shared last week—about justice rolling down like waters. Father often preached on it, but I've been developing my own understanding."

She carefully opened her journal to a page filled with her neat handwriting. "I believe justice isn't merely punishment for wrongdoing, but the restoration of dignity to those from whom it's been stolen. The mill children aren't simply unfortunate; they've been robbed of their childhood."

William's expression softened as he studied her words. "Your perspective has remarkable depth, Alice. You've moved beyond reciting theological principles to applying them to our present circumstances."

"It helps to have someone who listens," she admitted, her voice barely audible. "Sometimes I feel as though Father's death silenced me as well."

William leaned slightly closer, his eyes reflecting genuine concern. "Your voice matters, Alice. Your observations about the Pullmans' selective reading of Scripture revealed more insight than many scholars I encountered at Cambridge."

Alice felt something uncoil within her chest—a tightness she hadn't realised she'd been carrying. "I miss discussing these ideas openly. Father and I would talk for hours about how Christ's teachings should transform how we treat the vulnerable."

"Tell me more about him," William encouraged, pulling a chair slightly closer to hers while maintaining a respectful distance.

Alice found herself sharing memories she'd kept locked away —her father's gentle humour, his unwavering integrity, the way he'd taught her to see God's presence in unexpected places. William listened intently, asking thoughtful questions that allowed her grief space to breathe rather than demanding it retreat.

Later that night, Alice wrote in her journal by candlelight, her heart lighter than it had been in months:

Dear Providence,

I've found someone who sees me—truly sees me—as Father once did. Through our conversations, William has helped me realise that my thoughts aren't merely echoes of Father's teachings, but my own voice emerging. Perhaps this connection is Your answer to my prayers for purpose. I still carry Father's wisdom, but now I understand it isn't merely something to preserve but to build upon. Whatever path lies ahead, I feel less alone walking it.

JOURNAL

The dim glow of a single oil lamp cast long, flickering shadows across the library walls. William sat hunched at the heavy wooden table, quill scratching against parchment as he prepared lessons for Edgar. The boy had shown surprising aptitude for mathematics once properly engaged. Perhaps there was hope for him yet.

William paused, stretching his cramped fingers. The vast room felt different at night—more intimate somehow, despite its grandeur. Shelves of leather-bound volumes loomed like silent sentinels, their spines glinting gold in the lamplight.

He reached for another reference text, his elbow catching the edge of a stack Alice had been organising earlier. The books shifted precariously before toppling. William lunged forward, managing to steady most of them, but a small volume slipped free, landing with a soft thud on the carpet.

He muttered to himself, bending to retrieve it.

The book was unlike the others—plainer, with a worn leather cover bearing no title. William turned it over in his hands, noting its modest craftsmanship. When he opened it, his breath caught. He now recognised it.

This was no library book.

The pages were filled with neat, careful handwriting he recognised immediately as Alice's. His eyes fell upon the opening words: "Dear Providence..."

William knew he ought to close it straightaway. These were private thoughts, not meant for his eyes. Yet something in the earnestness of the words held him transfixed.

"Today marks six months since Father joined Mother in Heaven," he read. "Mr Pullman spoke harshly of Father during dinner, calling his concern for the mill children 'misguided sentimentality.' Father taught me that You are a God of truth, even when truth brings discomfort..."

William's chest tightened. Page after page revealed Alice's innermost reflections—her grief, her theological questions, her observations of the Pullmans' household. The depth of her insight stunned him. Here was no simple servant girl, but a soul wrestling with profound matters of faith and justice.

Her words about her father's death brought a lump to William's throat. The ache of her loneliness leapt from the page, yet alongside it burned a quiet, stubborn hope that reminded him painfully of his own struggles.

Before he could reconsider, William took a scrap of paper from his pocket. His quill hovered momentarily before he wrote: *These words deserve to be read. Faith speaks most clearly through honest questions.—W.*

He tucked the note carefully between the pages, then closed the journal with reverent hands. These weren't merely the scribbles of a lonely girl—they were testament to a remarkable mind that deserved encouragement, not silence.

~

Alice entered the library the following morning, her fingers still aching from scrubbing the kitchen floor. The household had already settled into its daily rhythm—Lavinia practicing piano with theatrical sighs, Edgar and William had decided to study in the garden today, and Mr Pullman had gone to the mill. She'd come to dust the shelves, a task that once felt like punishment but had transformed into a sanctuary since William's arrival.

Then she saw it.

Her journal—her private confessions to Providence—lay exposed upon the mahogany table where she'd carelessly left it the previous evening. Not tucked beneath the floorboard in her attic room. Not hidden inside her apron pocket. But here, vulnerable and unprotected in the one room William frequented most. She must have accidentally left it here after her last conversation with William.

The blood drained from Alice's face. She rushed forward, snatching the leather-bound book and clutching it to her chest as though it might disappear. Had anyone seen it? Had anyone read it? Had William—

Her fingers trembled as she opened the cover, scanning for signs of intrusion. The pages felt different somehow, as though they'd been disturbed by hands not her own. Then she saw it—a slip of paper that hadn't been there before, tucked between pages filled with her most intimate thoughts about her father's death, her theological questions, her observations of the Pullmans.

These words deserve to be read. Faith speaks most clearly through honest questions.—W

Alice's knees weakened. He had read her words—her private communion with Providence. The very thought made her stomach clench with mortification. What must he think of her? A servant girl with pretensions of theological understanding? A charity case who dared critique her benefactors?

She paced the narrow space between bookshelves, her heart hammering against her ribs. This invasion felt worse than Lavinia's mockery or Mr. Pullman's condescension. William had seemed different—someone who saw her as a person rather than a position. Now he'd peered into her soul without permission.

Alice squared her shoulders. She would confront him. Demand to know why he'd read what wasn't meant for his eyes. Father had always taught her that truth required courage, especially when facing those with power over you.

She slipped the journal into her apron pocket and straightened the dust cloth in her hand. William would be finished with Edgar's lessons soon. She would wait, and then she would speak.

A NEW OPPORTUNITY

Following the narrow path that led to the small stream bordering the Pullman property, Alice slipped through the garden gates, She'd overheard Mrs Reynolds telling the cook that Master Edgar had finished his lessons early, and William had taken his half-day liberty. Something pulled her toward the water, an instinct that proved correct when she spotted him sitting on a flat stone by the bank.

The afternoon sun dappled through the leaves, casting golden light across the scene. William sat with a small sketchbook balanced on his knee, pencil moving in swift, sure strokes across the page. The stream gurgled cheerfully, wildflowers nodded in the breeze, and butterflies danced above the water—all of it a cruel contrast to the storm raging inside her.

Alice's fingers tightened around her journal in her pocket. She stepped forward, snapping a twig beneath her worn boot. William looked up, his expression shifting from surprise to recognition.

"You found my journal, didn't you?" The words tumbled out before she could soften them, her voice tight with accusation.

William set his pencil down carefully. His face showed no

defensiveness, only a calm acknowledgment that somehow made her anger harder to maintain.

"I did," he said simply. "I knocked over your books while reaching for a mathematics text. It fell open, and I..." He paused, meeting her eyes directly. "I apologise, Miss Wells. I had no right to read what wasn't meant for me. I invaded your privacy, and I can only ask your forgiveness."

Alice stood rigid, clutching her apron with trembling fingers. "Those words were private. They were for Providence alone."

"I understand." William's voice softened. "I lost my father recently, after years of illness. His practice failed because he treated too many patients who couldn't pay." He looked toward the water. "I found myself writing letters to him after he was gone. No one was meant to read those either."

The parallel struck Alice with unexpected force. Her shoulders loosened slightly.

"Your reflections have remarkable depth," William continued. "Rather than hiding them away, I believe you should continue writing—refine your voice. Words can be both shelter and light in darkness."

"What use are words from someone like me?" Alice asked, though the bitterness in her voice had faded.

"Great use," William said firmly. "I could teach you proper composition, if you wished. In secret, of course. Your thoughts deserve to be expressed with the clarity and beauty they contain."

Alice's heart quickened. "You would teach me? Truly?"

"I would be honoured." William smiled, gesturing to the stone beside him. "Tell me, have you read Wordsworth? His reflections on nature remind me of your observations about the churchyard roses."

As Alice hesitantly sat beside him, they began exchanging thoughts about literature and faith. William listened intently to her interpretations of biblical passages, offering perspectives that complemented rather than corrected her own. Their conversation flowed with surprising ease, each discovery of shared understanding bridging the gulf between their stations.

William watched her animation grow as she spoke of her father's sermons, a protective warmth spreading through his chest. Here was a mind that deserved nurturing, a spirit that needed defending against the casual cruelties of the Pullman household.

WAITING FOR SOMEONE TO LISTEN

Alice hurried along the garden path, clutching a small bundle of papers beneath her shawl. The early autumn air carried a hint of crispness that hadn't been present during their summer meetings. For three months now, she and William had been meeting twice weekly—weather permitting—beneath the sprawling oak tree that stood sentinel at the far corner of the Pullman estate.

Their chosen spot remained hidden from the main house by a gentle rise in the land and a cluster of ornamental shrubs. Alice had learned of its perfect seclusion from Thomas during their garden conversations, though she'd never revealed to the kindly gardener why she valued this knowledge so dearly.

As the massive oak came into view, its leaves beginning to turn amber around the edges, Alice felt the familiar flutter in her chest—part scholarly anticipation, part something deeper she dared not name. William was already there, arranging a worn woollen blanket over the uneven ground.

"You're early today," she called softly, approaching with quickened steps.

"The young master was particularly disinterested in Euclid

this morning." William smiled, the corners of his eyes crinkling. "We finished sooner than expected."

Alice arranged herself carefully on the blanket, smoothing her faded grey dress beneath her. The fabric was worn thin at the knees from scrubbing floors, but here, beneath the oak's protective canopy, such things mattered less. Here, her mind—not her station—determined her worth.

"I've brought my latest composition," she said, unfolding her papers with careful fingers. "It's an analysis of Psalm 94, examining the call for divine justice against oppressors."

William's eyebrows rose appreciatively. "A challenging text. How have you connected it to our discussion of Milton last week?"

Their conversations had evolved over the months, from hesitant exchanges to rich dialogues where faith and literature intertwined. William posed questions that challenged rather than tested, creating space for Alice's thoughts to unfold naturally.

"I've considered how both texts wrestle with human suffering permitted by a just God," Alice explained, her voice growing stronger as she spoke. "Though Milton frames it through Satan's rebellion, while the psalmist confronts injustice directly."

As they debated interpretations, Alice marvelled at how her journal had transformed. Once merely a repository for private grief, it now brimmed with questions, analyses, and carefully constructed arguments. William had taught her to refine her natural insights with structure and precision, without diminishing their emotional truth.

"Your writing has such clarity now," William observed, handing back her pages. "You've found your voice."

Alice traced her finger along the edge of her composition. "It was always there, I suppose. Just waiting for someone to listen."

AUTUMN LEAVES

Alice sat beneath the oak tree, watching William's hands as he gestured enthusiastically about Paradise Lost. These lessons had transformed into something she treasured beyond measure—not merely instruction, but true intellectual companionship. She found herself laughing more freely than she had since Father died, their debates spirited yet respectful, their literary musings like secret treasures exchanged between equals.

"But don't you think Milton's Eve deserves more credit?" Alice challenged, leaning forward. "She sought knowledge, not merely disobedience."

William's eyes lit with that familiar spark that appeared whenever she presented an unexpected perspective. "An excellent point. The pursuit of understanding, even at great cost—there's courage in that, isn't there?"

Alice nodded, feeling that peculiar warmth spread through her chest. It happened increasingly often during their meetings—this strange, intoxicating pull toward him that both frightened and exhilarated her. She found herself noticing details she shouldn't: the way sunlight caught in his dark hair, how his voice softened when speaking of things that moved him deeply, the gentle respect in his eyes when considering her thoughts.

These feelings were dangerous, she knew. A dependent in the Pullman household couldn't afford such luxuries of the heart. Yet she found herself counting hours between their meetings, rehearsing clever observations that might earn his approving smile.

"This passage here," William said, pointing to a theological text they'd been examining. "Augustine speaks of divine love as something that transforms the soul. What do you make of his—"

A crisp autumn leaf, brilliant red-gold, drifted down between them, landing softly in Alice's hair. Absorbed in the discussion, she absently brushed at it, her attention fixed on the text.

William reached out instinctively, his fingers grazing her hair as he removed the leaf. "You missed it," he said, his voice suddenly lower.

Alice froze at the contact. The brief touch of his fingers against her hair sent something like lightning through her body. Their eyes met, and the world around them seemed to still.

Neither spoke. The moment stretched between them, heavy with unacknowledged feeling. Alice saw in William's expression a mirror of her own conflict—desire warring with propriety, connection tempered by circumstance. The oak leaves rustled overhead, as if whispering warnings about the impossibility of what hung in the air between a Cambridge-educated tutor and an orphaned dependent.

As autumn deepened, Alice found herself counting the remaining lessons before William would return to Cambridge. Each meeting became precious, tinged with the bittersweet knowledge of their coming separation. She stored away every shared insight, every approving nod, every moment their minds connected across the divide of their stations, like treasures to sustain her through the winter to come.

PAGES OF TRUTH

Alice's heart raced as William approached on their final day together. Golden autumn sunlight filtered through the branches, casting dappled patterns across the grass. He carried something in his hands—a small, leather-bound notebook that caught the light as he moved.

"I've brought you something," William said, his voice soft as he extended the gift toward her.

Alice hesitated before accepting it, knowing such a present far exceeded what was appropriate between them. The leather felt smooth beneath her fingers, the binding expertly crafted.

"I noticed your journal was getting quite full." He smiled. "So I thought you would need a new place for your thoughts."

Alice opened the cover with trembling fingers. Inside, William's neat handwriting filled the first page: *"For truths too precious to hide beneath floorboards. I shall think of you when the chapel bells ring."*

Her throat tightened. The words blurred before her eyes as she struggled to maintain composure. In this simple gift, William had acknowledged not just her mind, but her very existence—her worth beyond her station in the household. Not since Father died had anyone truly seen her this way.

"I don't know what to say," Alice whispered, her fingers tracing the edges of the pristine pages. Joy and sorrow battled within her—joy at being so perfectly understood, sorrow knowing their time together was ending. Each blank page represented possibility, yet reminded her of the coming emptiness of days without their discussions.

William watched her carefully, his expression revealing that he understood the weight of the moment. "The pages are waiting for your voice, Alice. A voice that deserves to be heard."

As their lesson drew to its inevitable close, silence fell between them. Words seemed inadequate for all that remained unsaid. The oak leaves rustled overhead, nature filling the void they couldn't bridge.

"Your guidance has meant more than I can express," Alice finally said, clutching the notebook to her chest. "You've helped me find my thoughts again when I feared they were lost forever."

"You've always had them," William replied, his voice steady despite the emotion in his eyes. "I merely provided the space for them to grow. Remember that, Alice. Your mind is your own, regardless of your circumstances."

After William walked away, Alice remained beneath the oak, watching his figure grow smaller as he returned to the manor. The notebook pressed against her heart like a talisman. Autumn leaves spiralled down around her, golden and crimson against the blue sky.

"*Providence*," she whispered, her prayer carried on the breeze, "*help me be worthy of this faith he's placed in me. Let these pages hold the truths my father taught me to seek.*"

UNWANTED ATTENTION

Alice moved quietly through the halls of Pullman Manor, painfully aware of how she'd changed since arriving as a grief-stricken fourteen-year-old. Now nineteen, her once angular frame had softened in a way that even the drab grey dresses Mrs Pullman insisted upon couldn't fully disguise. Her chestnut hair, pulled back severely from her face as befitted her station, nonetheless caught the light as she passed the tall windows overlooking the garden.

She paused before a mirror in the corridor, momentarily startled by her own reflection. The girl who had arrived five years ago—all knobby elbows and sorrow-filled eyes—had vanished. In her place stood a young woman with a quiet dignity that somehow transcended her circumstances. Alice quickly lowered her gaze, uncomfortable with this unwelcome transformation that seemed to draw attention wherever she went.

"Did you see her?" came a whisper as she passed the drawing room where Lavinia entertained guests. "The charity case has grown quite... noticeable."

"Quite," replied another voice, tinged with disdain. "One

wonders if keeping such a pretty face among the servants is entirely... prudent. But do tell me, how is the engagement, dear Lavinia!"

Alice quickened her pace, clutching her dusting cloth more tightly. These whispers had grown more frequent of late—some admiring, others suspicious, all unwanted. She longed for the invisibility she'd once possessed.

"Miss Wells."

The voice froze her mid-step. Mr Grimsby stood at the bottom of the staircase, his substantial frame blocking her path to the upper floors. His grey eyes traveled slowly from her face downward before returning to meet her gaze.

"You've managed the household accounts with remarkable efficiency," he said, stepping closer than propriety demanded. "Such skills would serve a woman well in managing her own household someday."

"Thank you, sir," Alice replied, keeping her tone neutral while taking a half-step backward. "I merely do what's required of me."

"Indeed." Grimsby's smile didn't reach his eyes. "A woman of your... capabilities... deserves security. At your age, without family connections, one must consider practical arrangements for the future."

His fingers brushed against her wrist as he reached to take the dusting cloth from her hand. "Perhaps we might discuss such arrangements. I find myself in need of a practical woman to oversee my household."

Alice withdrew her hand, fighting to keep her expression placid despite the chill that ran through her. "Excuse me, Mr Grimsby. Mrs Pullman expects these tasks completed before dinner."

Later, safe in her attic room, Alice's pen moved frantically across the pages of the journal William had given her years before.

. . .

Dear Providence,

Mr Grimsby cornered me again today. His words speak of security, but his eyes promise captivity. Each suggestion of marriage feels like a noose tightening. What choice have I but to endure his attentions? Without means or connections, where would I go? The walls of Pullman Manor, once merely cold, now feel increasingly dangerous.

~

Alice also noticed a shift in Lavinia's demeanour. At first, Alice thought little of it—Lavinia had always regarded her with contempt. But this was different. This was calculation.

"Alice, the silver needs polishing before tonight's gathering," Lavinia announced, though Alice had polished it just yesterday. "And the drawing room curtains must be taken down and beaten. The dust is simply intolerable."

"Yes, Miss Pullman," Alice replied, keeping her eyes downcast.

Lavinia lingered, twisting her engagement ring—a gaudy diamond that caught the light with every movement. "Lord Harrington and his family will be attending. Everything must be perfect." Her gaze slid to where Mr Grimsby stood across the hall, his attention fixed on Alice rather than the ledger in his hands.

The party that evening proved Lavinia's true intentions. Alice had barely finished the impossible list of tasks when guests began arriving. Her hands were raw from scrubbing, her back aching as she stood against the wall, ready to serve.

"The charity case will assist with wine service tonight," Lavinia announced to Mrs Reynolds, loud enough for nearby guests to hear. "Father insists we give her useful skills."

Alice moved through the crowded dining room, carefully

filling crystal glasses. She approached Lord Harrington—Lavinia's fiancé—when she felt something catch her foot. Lavinia had extended her slipper just enough to trip her. Wine splashed across the tablecloth, narrowly missing the nobleman's sleeve.

"How clumsy!" Lavinia exclaimed with mock concern. "Perhaps manual labor isn't suited to everyone after all."

Laughter rippled around the table. Alice's cheeks burned as she attempted to blot the spill.

"That's quite enough, Lavinia," Edgar's voice cut through the tittering. At eighteen, his voice had deepened, and he stood taller than his sister now. "Your behaviour is beneath you."

"I was merely observing—"

"You were deliberately cruel," Edgar interrupted, rising from his chair. "Alice, please bring fresh linens. The fault wasn't yours."

Lavinia's face flushed with anger. "Since when do you defend servants?"

"Since you became too preoccupied with appearances to remember basic decency," Edgar replied, his gaze steady.

Alice straightened her shoulders, remembering her father's words from years ago: *True dignity comes not from how others treat you, but how you carry yourself in the face of it.* She met Edgar's eyes briefly, a silent thank you passing between them, before retrieving fresh linens with quiet composure.

Alice kept her eyes down, focusing on the linen napkin she pressed against the spilled wine. The crimson stain spread like a blooming rose across the pristine tablecloth. She felt the weight of every gaze in the room upon her back, heavy with judgment and amusement at her expense.

"I say, that was hardly sporting of you, dearest"

The voice cut through the murmurs. Lord Harrington—Lavinia's fiancé—had spoken. Alice glanced up to find him regarding Lavinia with a look of mild disapproval.

"I beg your pardon?" Lavinia's voice was tight, her smile frozen in place.

"The girl clearly tripped over your foot. I watched it happen." Lord Harrington dabbed his napkin at a droplet of wine that had landed near his plate. "Deliberate, I should think."

Lavinia's face turned a shade deeper than the wine. "Charles, you misunderstood. I was merely shifting in my chair when—"

"When you extended your foot precisely as she passed." Lord Harrington's tone remained pleasant, but his eyes had hardened. "Rather beneath you, as Master Edgar said, wouldn't you agree?"

The silence that followed was thick enough to cut with the silver butter knife that lay untouched beside Alice's hand.

"Come, Alice," Edgar said quietly, appearing at her side. "I'm sure Mrs Reynolds needs help in the kitchen."

Alice felt his hand at her elbow, gently guiding her away from the table.

"I'm not finished with her," Lavinia hissed, half-rising from her chair.

"I do believe you are, sweetheart. Leave her be." Lord Harrington replied, his voice carrying across the table.

Edgar steered Alice through the dining room doors, his grip firm but kind. In the corridor, he released her arm and exhaled slowly.

"I apologise for my sister," he said, his voice low. "She's been... difficult since her engagement."

"Thank you," Alice whispered, her cheeks still burning with humiliation.

"It's nothing." Edgar glanced back toward the dining room, where conversation had resumed at an unnaturally high volume. "Best make yourself scarce for the remainder of the evening. I'll tell Mrs Reynolds you're indisposed."

WITNESS

Alice stood in the shadowed corner of Mr Pullman's study, the silver tea service balanced carefully in her hands. She had become adept at making herself invisible—a skill that served her well in this household. The clock on the mantel showed half past ten, and the room smelled of cigar smoke and brandy as Mr Pullman and Mr Grimsby hunched over the massive oak desk.

"The inspector arrives next Tuesday," Mr Pullman muttered, his voice low but clear in the quiet room. "We cannot afford another citation after that business with the Pemberton boy's arm."

Mr Grimsby nodded, shuffling papers. "I've adjusted the maintenance records. According to these, we've replaced the safety guards on all the looms in the east wing."

"And the accident reports?"

"Reduced by half. I've recorded only the adults, none of the children. The rest are listed as... minor incidents requiring no medical attention."

Alice's hands trembled slightly, causing the china to rattle. Both men glanced up, and she quickly steadied herself.

"Just set it down, girl," Mr Pullman waved dismissively.

Alice placed the tray on the side table, her mind racing. She'd seen those children return from the mill—bloodied fingers, crushed hands, lungs ravaged by cotton dust. Minor incidents? She thought of little Mary Collins, just nine years old, who'd lost three fingers last month.

"The ledger shows we've spent considerable sums on improvements," Mr Grimsby continued once Alice stepped back. He tapped a column of numbers. "Of course, that money actually went to the Manchester expansion, but the inspector needn't know that."

Mr Pullman chuckled. "Excellent work, Grimsby. Those bleeding-heart reformers can wave their Factory Acts all they like. Business is business."

Alice felt bile rise in her throat. She backed toward the door, desperate to escape before her face betrayed her. The falsified books, the deliberate deception—it wasn't just dishonesty. It was murder by neglect.

"You're dismissed," Mr Pullman said without looking up.

Alice fled upstairs to her attic room, her heart hammering against her ribs. She paced the small space, hands pressed against her mouth to stifle the scream building inside her. Children would die because of those falsified records. More would be maimed, their small bodies sacrificed for Pullman's profits.

With shaking hands, she retrieved her journal from beneath the floorboard and began to write:

Dear Providence,

Tonight I witnessed something that has shaken me to my core. Mr Pullman and Mr Grimsby have falsified the mill's safety records to deceive inspectors. They speak of children's injuries as if discussing spoiled inventory. Father always said that truth must be spoken, even when it brings discomfort. But what can I do with this truth?

I am torn between silence and the truth. I know what I heard could destroy the Pullman empire, yet I feel powerless as a mere girl under the Pullmans' roof. If I speak out, where would I go? Who would believe me against the word of Silas Pullman? Yet if I remain silent, am I not complicit in whatever harm befalls those children?

Father, I wish you were here to guide me. You would know how to wield truth like a sword of righteousness. I have only a pen and my conscience.

Alice closed her journal and moved to the window. Outside, the moon cast silver light across the grounds of Pullman Manor. Somewhere beyond those manicured hedges were the cramped cottages where mill workers lived—where children slept fitfully before another day of danger.

She pressed her palm against the cold glass. Her words in this journal were both confession and testimony. Whatever came next, she would continue to write, to bear witness. In a house built on lies, perhaps truth was the only rebellion possible.

RETURN

William gripped the reins more firmly as the familiar Yorkshire hills came into view. His final years at Cambridge had transformed him from an idealistic youth into a man with purpose, his shoulders broader, his jaw more defined. At twenty-three, he carried himself with the quiet confidence of someone who had earned his place in the world.

A small school awaited him in the neighbouring town—his first position as headmaster. Pride swelled in his chest at the thought, yet it was not this accomplishment that quickened his pulse as he approached the crossroads. It was the memory of earnest brown eyes and a mind sharper than any he'd encountered at university.

Alice Wells. Her name whispered through his thoughts like a prayer.

He turned his horse toward Pullman Manor instead of his new lodgings. The excuse of expressing gratitude for his former position would suffice, though William harboured no illusions about his true purpose. He needed to see her again.

The manor loomed ahead, more imposing than he remembered. Grey stone walls stretched upward, windows like watchful eyes. William dismounted, straightening his coat and adjusting his collar before approaching the entrance.

"Mr Thornton, what a surprise." Silas Pullman's voice boomed across the entrance hall. "Come to show us what Cambridge has made of you, have you?"

"Good afternoon, Mr Pullman." William bowed slightly. "I've returned to take a position at Hargrove School. I thought it proper to pay my respects to your family, given the opportunity you once provided me."

Silas's handshake was firm to the point of discomfort. "Headmaster now, is it? Quite the advancement for a young man."

"A modest establishment, sir, but one with potential."

William's gaze swept the room, noting Lavinia perched on a settee, her lips pursed in displeasure. She'd grown more refined in his absence, yet her eyes held the same cold calculation he remembered.

"Miss Pullman, you're looking well." He nodded in her direction.

"Cambridge hasn't improved your fashion sense, I see." Her smile didn't reach her eyes.

William forced a polite laugh. "Some matters of importance transcend appearance."

Movement in the doorway caught his attention. Grimsby entered, his heavy footsteps marking his presence before he spoke.

"Ah, the tutor returns." Grimsby's voice carried a sneer. "Though I hear you've risen in station. Not quite as high as some of us, but commendable nonetheless."

William's jaw tightened. "Mr Grimsby."

The way Grimsby's eyes darted toward the hallway—expectant, hungry—made William's stomach turn. He'd heard whispers about Grimsby's intentions toward Alice, and the predatory glint in the man's eyes confirmed his worst fears.

"I wonder if I might pay my respects to all members of the household," William said carefully. "Including Miss Wells. I understand she remains under your care."

"The charity case?" Lavinia laughed. "Whatever for?"

"Professional courtesy," William replied evenly. "As an educator, I take interest in the development of all young minds I've encountered."

Before departing, William managed to speak briefly with Edgar, slipping him a folded note. "For Miss Wells," he whispered. "Tell her I'll wait at her father's church at sunset." Edgar's eyebrows raised at being so trusted, but a look of determination set on his face.

As he mounted his horse, William's heart hammered against his ribs. The parish church stood silent in the distance, its spire reaching toward heaven—a fitting place to offer Alice the promise of protection he'd carried across the miles between them.

ONE YEAR

Alice hurried through the gathering dusk, her heart pounding with each step toward the parish church. The note from William had been brief but clear—he urgently wished to speak with her. She slipped through the churchyard, memories of her father washing over her as she passed the graves. How many times had they walked these paths together, discussing Scripture and the nature of faith?

The heavy wooden door creaked as she pushed it open. Inside, the church stood transformed by evening shadows, a handful of candles casting dancing light across the worn stone walls. The familiar smell of beeswax and old prayer books enveloped her, and Alice felt her shoulders drop, tension melting away like snow in spring. After the suffocating atmosphere of Pullman Manor, the church's quiet sanctuary wrapped around her like an embrace.

William stood near the altar, his tall figure silhouetted against the candlelight. When he turned, his face illuminated with relief and something deeper that made Alice's breath catch.

"You came," he said simply.

"Of course I did."

Their eyes met across the empty nave, and in that moment, Alice felt understood without speaking a word. William crossed the distance between them with purposeful strides.

"I've thought of you every day at Cambridge," he began, his voice low and urgent. "Your situation at Pullman Manor—it troubles me deeply. Especially now that I've seen how Grimsby looks at you."

Alice's carefully maintained composure cracked. "He corners me when no one is watching. Speaks of marriage as though I should be grateful for his interest." Her voice trembled. "And Lavinia—she's grown more vicious since her engagement. Last week she deliberately caused me to spill wine before all their guests."

The words tumbled out, months of suffering finally finding voice. She told him about the falsified mill records, the children's injuries hidden from inspectors, and her growing fear that she would never escape.

William listened intently, his expression darkening. When she finished, he took her hands in his, his touch warm and steady.

"Listen to me, Alice. I am establishing myself now. Give me one year to secure my position, and I will find a way for you to leave this house with your reputation intact."

The promise hung between them, tangible as the stone walls surrounding them. Alice felt something unfurl in her chest—hope, fragile but persistent.

"One year," she whispered.

"I won't abandon you to this fate," William said, his voice thick with emotion. "You deserve so much more than to be someone's charity case or Grimsby's convenient wife."

As they stood together in the flickering light, William slowly leaned forward. His lips brushed against her forehead, gentle as a prayer. Though chaste, the gesture sent warmth cascading through Alice's body, a silent acknowledgment of feelings neither dared name aloud.

"Continue writing," he whispered against her skin. "Your words to Providence will sustain you until we meet again."

Alice's eyes locked with his, finding strength in his unwavering gaze. "I will," she promised.

After William had gone, Alice remained in the empty church, her fingers tracing the spot where his lips had touched her skin. For the first time since her father's death, she felt truly seen—not as an obligation or a servant, but as herself.

That night, Alice wrote in her journal with renewed purpose, her mother's Bible open beside her. William's promise nestled in her heart like a small flame, illuminating the darkness around her.

DISASTER AT THE MILL

The sky brooded over Pullman's mill like a judge awaiting sentence. Mary tugged her threadbare shawl tighter round her shoulders as she trudged towards the looming brick structure that had swallowed half her childhood. At thirteen, she'd already worked there six years, fingers calloused from the constant threading and repairing of broken cotton strands, lungs perpetually tight from breathing lint-filled air.

"Looks like rain again," muttered Betsy beside her, a girl of ten with haunted eyes and a persistent cough. "Roof'll leak something terrible today."

Mary nodded, noting the dark patches spreading across the western wall where water had seeped through the brickwork for months. Mr. Grimsby had dismissed complaints about it, claiming repairs would halt production. The foreman's exact words still rang in Mary's ears: "Mills don't make money standing idle, girl."

Inside, the familiar cacophony engulfed her—the thunderous clacking of looms, the whirring of spindles, the shouted instructions barely audible above the mechanical din. Children darted between massive machines, their small bodies perfect for reaching into tight spaces adults couldn't access.

"They're pushing harder today," Tom whispered as he passed, his face grey with exhaustion. "Boss says we're behind schedule."

Mary glanced up at the wooden beams supporting the ceiling. They'd been creaking more lately, especially when the machines ran at full tilt. A dark stain spread across one beam where water had been dripping steadily since yesterday's downpour.

"Something don't feel right," said old Samuel, who'd worked the mills for forty years. Nobody paid him mind. Samuel always said something didn't feel right.

The overseer's whistle pierced the air, signaling increased speed. The machines responded, their rhythm intensifying, vibrations traveling through the floorboards beneath Mary's feet. The walls seemed to tremble with each rotation of the great wheel that powered the factory.

Then came the sound—a sharp crack like a gunshot, followed by an ominous groan from somewhere overhead.

"The beam!" Samuel shouted, pointing upward.

Mary looked up as the massive wooden support splintered. Time slowed. Children scattered like startled birds. The machinery continued its relentless pace, oblivious to human panic.

The roof collapsed inward with a deafening roar, bringing down walls and machinery in a cascade of brick, wood, and iron. Mary felt herself thrown backward by the force, her ears filled with screaming. Dust billowed outward in thick clouds, choking, blinding.

When Mary could see again, half the mill lay in ruins. Where the spinning frames had stood moments before, there was only rubble. Small figures lay motionless beneath fallen beams while others crawled from the wreckage, faces streaked with blood and dust.

"Betsy!" Mary screamed, scrambling toward where she'd last seen the small girl. "Tom!"

All around her, workers clawed desperately at the debris, pulling free those they could reach. A high, thin wailing rose from beneath a collapsed section of wall—the unmistakable sound of a child in agony.

INFIRMARY

The commotion erupted without warning. Shouts echoed through the manor's halls, followed by the pounding of urgent footsteps. Alice paused in her dusting of the parlour when Mr Pullman's voice boomed from the entrance hall.

"Bring them around to the back! Straight to the kitchen—and keep it quiet!"

Alice moved to the window. A cluster of men carried small, limp figures toward the servants' entrance. Blood stained their clothing. Her stomach lurched at the sight of a child's arm dangling motionless.

"Mill accident," whispered a passing maid. "Roof collapsed."

Alice's heart hammered against her ribs as she rushed down the servants' staircase. The kitchen had been transformed into a makeshift infirmary, tables cleared of food and covered with sheets. Mrs. Reynolds directed kitchen maids to boil water while Mr. Pullman spoke in hushed tones with Mr. Grimsby.

"Not a word to the inspector," he muttered. "We'll handle this ourselves."

Edgar stood near the door, his face ashen as he watched the

procession of injured children. His eyes met Alice's across the room.

"We need clean linens," Alice called out, instinctively taking charge. "And spirits for the wounds."

She gathered scissors, needle and thread from Mrs. Reynolds' mending basket. Her hands trembled slightly as she tore strips of cloth for bandages. The door burst open again as two men carried in a small girl, her face grey with dust and pain.

Alice froze. "Mary?"

The child's eyes fluttered open at the sound of her name. Blood seeped through her sleeve where a jagged piece of wood had pierced her arm.

"Miss Wells?" Mary whispered.

Alice knelt beside her. "I'm here. You're going to be all right."

She recognised Mary instantly—the daughter of Mrs Pemberton who had once kept house for her father. Alice had often played with Mary when her mother came to help at the parsonage.

"Let me see your arm," Alice murmured, gently cutting away the torn sleeve. The wound was deep but clean. She worked methodically, washing away dirt and blood before binding the injury with steady hands.

"The beam just... gave way," Mary whispered through chattering teeth. "Tom was right beside me and then... he wasn't."

Alice draped a blanket over the shivering child. "Shh, don't try to talk now."

"No," Mary clutched Alice's wrist with surprising strength. "Things have worsened since the kind reverend stopped coming to the mill."

The words struck Alice like a physical blow. Her father had regularly visited the mill, speaking with workers, observing conditions. She remembered his notebooks filled with careful documentation of safety concerns.

"Father knew," Alice whispered, more to herself than to Mary. "He knew how dangerous it was."

Mary's eyelids drooped as exhaustion claimed her. "He tried to help us. Nobody listens now."

Understanding bloomed painfully in Alice's chest. Her father hadn't simply been preaching abstract morality—he'd been fighting a specific battle against negligence that had now resulted in this carnage. Without his advocacy, conditions had deteriorated to the point of disaster.

She turned away, focusing on bandaging another child's lacerated hand, her movements precise despite the rage building within her.

"I'll listen," she whispered to Mary. "And I won't stay silent."

The kitchen door banged open as Silas Pullman strode in, surveying the makeshift infirmary with narrowed eyes. His gaze swept over the injured children without lingering on any single face, as though they were damaged inventory rather than suffering human beings.

"Get these brats cleaned up quickly," he barked at Mrs Reynolds. "I've sent word to their families. They'll be collected by nightfall."

Alice continued wrapping a bandage around a small boy's wrist, her hands steady despite the fury building within her.

"And for Pete's sake, keep them quiet," Silas continued, straightening his waistcoat. "Lord Harrington is still in the drawing room. The last thing we need is him hearing this commotion and asking questions."

"Some of them need a proper doctor, sir," Alice said, her voice low but clear.

Silas turned his cold eyes upon her. "And who'll pay for that, Miss Wells? Their families? The mill's had a setback as it is."

"A setback?" The word escaped Alice's lips before she could stop it. "Children are injured."

"Accidents happen in industry," Silas replied dismissively.

"We've provided immediate care, which is more than most would do. Their parents signed agreements acknowledging the risks."

Alice's stomach churned with disgust as she watched him adjust his cufflinks, more concerned with his appearance than the blood-stained children before him.

"I expect this matter to be handled with discretion," he announced to the room. "There's no need for exaggerated accounts to reach the village. The situation is unfortunate but entirely unavoidable."

Alice bit her tongue so hard she tasted blood. Unavoidable. The word mocked everything her father had stood for, everything he had warned about.

"Mr Grimsby," Silas called as he turned to leave, "prepare a statement for the parish gazette. Something appropriate about our swift response to an unforeseen structural issue."

When the last injured child had been collected, Alice climbed the stairs to her attic room, her skirts spattered with blood and her mind haunted by Mary's words. She lit her single candle with trembling hands and retrieved her journal from beneath the floorboard.

Dear Providence, she wrote, her pen pressing hard against the page.

Today I witnessed the consequence of silence. Children broken because men like Silas Pullman value profit above life. Mary Pemberton told me conditions worsened after Father stopped visiting the mill. His voice was extinguished, and this is the result—splintered bones and torn flesh.

I have been writing in these pages as though they were merely a sanctuary, a place to preserve my thoughts. But Father didn't just think or pray about injustice—he acted. He spoke. He documented.

. . .

Alice paused, tears blurring her vision as clarity settled over her.

These pages must become more than my refuge. They must become my testimony. Father kept records of the mill's conditions. Perhaps those notes still exist somewhere in his Bible or papers. I will find them. I will continue his work.

The truth cannot remain hidden beneath floorboards and behind closed doors. I will be a voice for Mary and all the others. I will honour Father's memory not just through remembrance but through action.

THE SPINE

Alice closed her journal and slid it back beneath the loose floorboard. Sleep would not come easily tonight, not with the memory of broken children still fresh in her mind. She reached for her mother's Bible, the leather binding worn smooth from years of devoted handling. In the dim light of her single candle, shadows danced across the attic walls, making the small space feel even more isolated.

She pulled the Bible onto her lap and sat cross-legged on her thin mattress. The familiar weight of it against her knees offered a comfort nothing else could provide. Alice traced her fingers over her mother's handwriting in the margins, seeking solace in the connection to her parents.

"Show me what to do," she whispered, turning the pages slowly, reverently.

As she leafed through Psalms, something about the binding caught her attention. The leather cover seemed thicker than it should be at the back. Alice turned the Bible over, examining it more carefully. There, almost imperceptible unless one was looking for it, was a slight bulge in the spine's lining.

Her heart quickened. With trembling fingers, she carefully

worked at the seam where the leather had been subtly stitched. The ancient glue gave way under her persistent touch, revealing a hidden pocket within the binding. Alice drew in a sharp breath as she extracted several folded papers, yellowed with age but preserved within their hiding place.

Her father's neat, precise handwriting filled the pages. Dates, times, locations within the mill. Lists of violations—inadequate supports in the east wing, machinery without proper guards, locked fire exits during working hours. Children assigned to dangerous tasks without training. Reports of previous injuries systematically ignored.

"Oh, Father," she whispered, her voice catching.

Alice's hands shook as she skimmed through the notes. They were meticulous, damning—a careful documentation of every safety violation Pullman had dismissed. Names of injured workers, ages of children working dangerous machinery, structural weaknesses that had been reported and ignored.

The mill collapse was no accident. It was negligence, pure and simple.

The weight of this discovery settled over her like a physical presence. These pages contained more than memories—they held evidence that could expose Pullman's disregard for human life. Evidence that could bring justice for Mary Pemberton and countless others.

Alice gathered the papers carefully, her mind racing. For years, she had felt powerless within these walls, reduced to nothing more than "the charity case." But now, holding her father's careful documentation, she felt something ignite within her—a fierce, burning determination.

The truth her father had died protecting was literally in her hands.

CONFRONTATION

Alice needed somewhere quiet to think, to plan her next steps.

The library seemed the obvious choice—at this hour, the family would be occupied elsewhere. Alice slipped through the manor's corridors, careful to avoid the main hallways where she might be spotted and assigned yet another meaningless task.

The heavy library door creaked as she pushed it open, and Alice winced at the sound. She stepped inside, relief washing over her at finding the room empty. The familiar smell of leather bindings and paper enveloped her as she moved toward the desk near the window. Perhaps she could make copies of some of the most damning evidence, a precaution should the originals be discovered, which she had safely stowed away within her hidden journal.

"Well, well. What brings you here at this hour, Miss Wells?"

Alice's blood ran cold. Mr Grimsby emerged from between two tall bookshelves, his grey eyes gleaming in the lamplight. She hadn't noticed him sitting in the shadowed corner, watching.

"I was just looking for a book to read before bed, sir." Alice backed toward the door.

"Curious timing." Grimsby moved with deliberate slowness, positioning himself between Alice and the exit. "I've been hoping for a moment alone with you."

The predatory smile that spread across his face made Alice's skin crawl. He stepped closer, forcing her to retreat until her back pressed against a bookshelf next to the desk.

"I've been thinking about your situation here." His voice dropped to what he clearly thought was an intimate tone. "A young woman with no family, no prospects. Your position is... precarious."

"I manage well enough, thank you." Alice tried to keep her voice steady, searching for an escape route.

"For now, perhaps." Grimsby's hand reached out to touch her cheek. Alice flinched away. "But what of your future? A practical arrangement between us would solve everything. As my wife, you would finally have security."

"Your wife?" Alice couldn't keep the horror from her voice.

"Don't sound so shocked." His smile hardened. "It's a generous offer for someone in your position. I'm rescuing you."

Alice's heart hammered against her ribs. His eyes roved over her in a way that made her feel physically ill. She glanced desperately around the room, spotting a silver letter opener on the desk just beside her.

"I don't need rescuing, Mr. Grimsby." Alice's hand closed around the letter opener, its weight cool against her palm. "And I must decline your... proposal."

"Decline?" Grimsby's face darkened. "You misunderstand. This isn't a request."

He lunged forward, reaching for her arm. Alice reacted without thinking, bringing the letter opener up between them. The sharp edge caught his sleeve, grazing the skin beneath.

Grimsby recoiled with a hiss of pain, clutching his arm where a thin line of red appeared.

He stared at her in shock, his face contorting with rage.

Alice stood firm, the letter opener still raised. Her hand trembled, but her voice did not.

"Do not touch me again, Mr Grimsby. EVER!"

Alice backed away from Grimsby, letter opener still clutched in her trembling hand. His expression had transformed from shock to something far more dangerous—a calculating fury that promised retribution.

"You'll regret this," he snarled, advancing toward her again. "Who do you think they'll believe? The respected business manager or the charity case?"

The library door flew open with a bang. Edgar stood in the doorway, his eyes widening as he took in the scene—Alice cornered, Grimsby's bleeding arm, the letter opener glinting in the lamplight.

"What's happening here?" Edgar's voice cracked slightly, but he stepped forward with unexpected resolve, placing himself between Alice and Grimsby.

"This doesn't concern you, boy," Grimsby spat. "Your father's ward has forgotten her place. She attacked me!"

"I saw enough," Edgar said, his voice steadier now. "And I heard enough too. You weren't proposing—you were threatening her."

Alice stared at Edgar in disbelief. The boy who had once tormented her alongside Lavinia now stood as her defender, shoulders squared against a man twice his age.

"You'd take her word over mine?" Grimsby's voice dropped dangerously.

"I would." Edgar didn't flinch. "And I'll tell Father exactly what I witnessed if you don't leave her alone."

A tense silence filled the room. Grimsby's eyes darted between them, calculating his options.

"This isn't finished," he finally muttered, pressing a handkerchief to his arm as he stalked toward the door. "Not by a long measure."

When the door closed behind him, Edgar turned to Alice. "Are you all right?"

Alice nodded, still clutching the letter opener. "Why did you help me?"

Edgar guided her toward the servants' staircase, checking first to ensure no one would see them. "We need to get you somewhere safe. He'll be back once he's composed himself."

As they hurried up the narrow stairs, Edgar spoke in hushed tones. "I've watched how he looks at you. It's been getting worse."

At the landing, he paused, a flush creeping up his neck. "I think I'm in love with you, Alice. Have been for some time. But I'm not a fool—I've seen how you look at William. Your heart belongs elsewhere."

Alice stared at Edgar, his confession hanging in the air between them. His features had changed so much since that first day she'd arrived at Pullman Manor—the cruel boy replaced by a young man with unexpected courage. She felt a rush of gratitude that nearly overwhelmed her.

"Thank you, Edgar." Her voice softened. "Not just for tonight, but for everything."

Edgar shifted uncomfortably under her gaze, but a small smile played at the corners of his mouth.

"I wasn't always kind to you," he admitted. "I regret that now."

Alice reached for his hand and squeezed it gently. "We were children then. What matters is who we choose to become."

Standing on tiptoe, she placed a gentle kiss on his cheek. Edgar's face flushed crimson, but his eyes shone with something like pride.

"You're going to make the right woman so happy one day."

"You should go to your room and lock the door," he said, suddenly businesslike. "I'll make sure Grimsby behaves himself. He won't dare make a scene with Father around, and by morning, he'll have convinced himself it's better to pretend nothing happened."

"Are you certain?" Alice whispered, glancing nervously down the darkened hallway.

"I am." Edgar straightened his shoulders. "Go now, quickly."

Alice hurried down the corridor to her attic room, her mind racing. The confrontation with Grimsby, Edgar's unexpected declaration—it was too much to process. She needed to write it all down, to make sense of it in her journal.

She closed her door, sliding the small bolt into place. The familiar creak of the floorboard as she crossed to her bed was oddly comforting. Alice knelt down and reached for the loose board where she kept her most precious possessions.

Her fingers found the empty space where her journal should have been.

Alice frantically pushed aside her mother's Bible and the leather-bound notebook from William, searching the small hiding place. But her journal—filled with her observations about the Pullmans, her private thoughts about William, and the papers that her father had gathered —all were gone.

BAD FOR BUSINESS

Alice slept fitfully, her dreams filled with shadowy figures rifling through her belongings. When dawn broke, she startled awake to three sharp knocks on her door.

"Miss Wells," came a stern voice, "your presence is required in Mr Pullman's office. Immediately."

Her heart hammered against her ribs as she dressed hastily. The worn floorboards creaked beneath her feet as she descended the servants' staircase, each step bringing her closer to whatever awaited below.

Mr Pullman's office door stood ajar. Alice paused, drawing a deep breath before entering. The room fell silent at her appearance. Silas Pullman sat behind his massive oak desk, his face impassive. Mr Grimsby stood to one side, his expression guarded. And there, positioned triumphantly beside her father, stood Lavinia, her lips curved in a satisfied smile.

On the desk before Silas lay Alice's journal, its worn leather cover unmistakable.

"Good morning, Miss Wells," Silas said, his voice deceptively calm. "It seems we have much to discuss."

Lavinia stepped forward, her silk morning dress rustling. "I was concerned about strange noises coming from your room," she said, her eyes glittering with malice. "Imagine my shock when I discovered this hidden beneath your floorboards."

Alice's mouth went dry. She glanced at Grimsby, who remained silent, his eyes fixed on a point above her head.

"I've taken the liberty of reading your... observations," Silas continued, tapping the journal with one thick finger. "Most disturbing. Delusions about my business. Accusations against this family that has charitably housed you. And these inappropriate exchanges with young Mr. Thornton—"

"They're private thoughts," Alice managed, her voice barely audible.

"Private madness, more like," Lavinia interjected. "Father, she's clearly unstable. A danger to our reputation—perhaps even to ourselves."

Silas nodded gravely. "Indeed." His eyes narrowed. "These are not merely the ravings of an unbalanced mind, but bad for business. These are falsified defamations." Silas wielded her father's papers. He tutted as he put them in the bottom draw of his desk. "The ramblings of a madwoman and her father…"

He closed the journal with deliberate slowness. "There are institutions for young women of unsound mind, Miss Wells. Places where such... disturbances can be properly managed."

The threat hung in the air like poison.

"Perhaps we should simply turn her out," Grimsby finally spoke.

"No," Lavinia said, her voice honeyed with false concern. "I have a better suggestion. The mill house is vacant since the overseer's departure. She could be kept there until arrangements are made. Away from prying eyes."

"An excellent suggestion," Silas agreed. "Until then, Miss Wells will remain confined to her room."

HELP

Alice sat motionless on her attic bed, the door now locked from the outside. The fading afternoon light cast long shadows across the floorboards where her journal had once been hidden.

Three sharp knocks on her door startled her from her thoughts. The key turned in the lock, and Edgar slipped inside, his face drawn with worry.

"I can't stay long," he whispered, glancing nervously over his shoulder. "They think I've gone to fetch a book from the library."

Alice rose, hope fluttering in her chest. "Edgar, I—"

"There's no time." He cut her off, his voice trembling. "I'm going to William. I've heard everything—Father plans to move you to the mill house around midnight, when everyone is asleep. From there..." He swallowed hard. "Grimsby has connections at an asylum in Leeds. Father has already sent a letter describing your 'condition'."

Alice's blood ran cold. She'd heard whispers about such places—women locked away for years, subjected to treatments more torturous than curative.

"Why are you helping me?" she asked, searching his face.

Edgar's eyes met hers, guilt and determination warring in their depths. "Because I've been a coward for too long. Your father showed me kindness once when no one else would. And because..." He hesitated. "Because it's the right thing to do."

He moved toward the door. "I'll find William tonight. Tell him everything."

"Be careful," Alice whispered. "If your father discovers—"

"Some things matter more than being a Pullman," Edgar replied, a new resolve straightening his shoulders. "I'll return if I can."

The door closed behind him, the key turning once more in the lock. Alice pressed her palms against her racing heart. In Edgar's face, she'd seen something she recognised—the same quiet courage her father had possessed. The courage to stand for truth, whatever the cost.

~

William paced the length of his modest quarters at the school, his mind churning with thoughts of Alice. The candlelight cast long shadows across the room as evening descended. Something felt wrong. He'd been unable to concentrate on his lessons all day, a sense of foreboding hanging over him like the Yorkshire mist.

A frantic pounding at his door broke the silence.

William flung it open to find Edgar Pullman standing there, rain-soaked and breathless. The young man's face was pale, his eyes wide with fear.

"Mr Thornton—" Edgar gasped, clutching the doorframe. "You must come quickly."

William pulled him inside. "Edgar? What's happened?"

"It's Alice," Edgar said, his voice breaking. "Lavinia found her journal and gave it to Father. They know everything—about her writing... About you."

William's blood ran cold. "Where is she now?"

"Locked in the attic." Edgar wiped rainwater from his face, his hands trembling. "Father means to move her to the old mill house tonight. It's just a temporary measure until-" He faltered.

"Until what?" William demanded, gripping Edgar's shoulders.

"Until he can arrange for her to be taken to an asylum in Leeds." Edgar's voice dropped to a whisper. "He's claiming she's of unsound mind, dangerous to our family. Lavinia's convinced him."

William turned away, running a hand through his hair. "How much time do we have?"

"Hours at most. They plan to move her after midnight when the servants are asleep." Edgar grabbed William's arm. "Please, Mr Thornton. I know I've been cruel to her in the past, but I cannot bear this injustice. She doesn't deserve this fate."

William saw genuine remorse in the young man's eyes—the same eyes that had once looked at Alice with disdain now filled with desperate concern.

"You're risking everything by coming here," William said quietly.

Edgar straightened his shoulders. "Some things are worth the risk."

ESCAPE

The faint glow of moonlight seeped through Alice's attic window, casting long shadows across the floorboards. She sat motionless on her bed, ears straining for any sound from the corridor. The house had fallen silent hours ago, but sleep remained impossible.

A soft scratching at the door made her breath catch. Three gentle taps followed—a signal.

"Alice?" William's voice, barely above a whisper, sent a flood of relief through her body.

The lock clicked and the door swung open. William stood there, his face half-hidden in shadow, with Edgar hovering anxiously behind him.

"We haven't much time," William said, stepping inside. "Mrs Reynolds has done her best to sneak us in and keep everything quiet, but it's only a matter of time."

Edgar pushed forward, pressing a familiar leather-bound book into her hands. "I took this from Father's office. It's yours."

Alice's fingers trembled as they closed around her journal. "Thank you."

William outlined their plan in hushed tones. "I've prepared a horse. We'll take the servants' stairs to avoid the main hall. Edgar will create a distraction if needed."

"If Father catches us—" Edgar began.

"He won't," William cut him off, his voice firm with resolve.

Alice clutched her journal, and Bible to her chest, feeling the worn leather against her fingers. William's presence filled the small attic room with a strange mix of urgency and calm. His eyes darted to the door as footsteps passed in a distant corridor.

"Listen carefully," William whispered, taking her hands in his. "If anything happens—if we're separated—you must find Mrs Bennett."

"Mrs Bennett?" Alice repeated, committing the name to memory.

William nodded. "She taught me at Cambridge, retired last year to a cottage in the nearby village. It's less than three miles east of here." His voice dropped lower. "She lives in a white cottage with blue shutters at the edge of the village, near the old oak. You can't miss it."

Alice nodded, her mind racing to absorb every detail.

"Mrs Bennett is someone you can trust completely," William continued, his thumbs brushing over her knuckles. "She was my mentor—knows more about justice and moral courage than anyone I've ever met. Tell her I sent you, and she'll help."

"Why would we be separated?" Alice asked, fear creeping into her voice.

William's expression darkened. "Pullman has connections—people watching the roads. If anything happens, don't wait for me. Go straight to Mrs Bennett."

Edgar shifted nervously by the door. "We need to move now."

William squeezed Alice's hands once more. "Promise me you'll remember—Mrs Bennett in Thornfield village. White cottage, blue shutters."

"I promise," Alice whispered, tucking the information away like a precious stone.

The thought of being separated from William after finding him again sent a chill through her, but Alice straightened her shoulders. She had survived almost six years in this house. She would not falter now when freedom was so close.

"Are you ready, Alice?" William asked.

Alice nodded. The corridors of Pullman Manor had never seemed so vast and threatening as they did now, stretching before her like the jaws of some great beast. Each creaking floorboard sent her heart racing. The walls that had imprisoned her for years now seemed to close in, watching their escape with malevolent eyes.

William led the way, his hand occasionally brushing hers in reassurance. The touch anchored her, keeping panic at bay. Edgar trailed behind, glancing nervously over his shoulder at every corner.

"Almost there," William whispered as they approached the servants' entrance.

A sudden shout from the main hall froze them in place.

"Check the grounds!" Silas Pullman's voice boomed through the house. "Grimsby, take the east wing!"

"They've discovered you're gone," Edgar hissed.

William pulled Alice into an alcove as heavy footsteps approached. "Change of plan. We'll use the front entrance—they'll be searching the back."

They darted across the main hall, keeping to the shadows. Freedom lay just beyond the heavy oak doors.

William reached for the handle, then jerked back as the doors burst open. Four of Pullman's men stood silhouetted against the night, Grimsby's sneering face visible among them.

"Well, well," Grimsby drawled. "What have we here?"

"Run!" William shouted, shoving Alice toward a side corridor as he lunged at Grimsby.

Edgar threw himself at another man, creating chaos in the narrow space. Bodies collided in the darkness, shouts echoing off the walls.

"Alice, go!" William called out as he wrestled with Grimsby.

A hand caught her arm, yanking her back. Alice twisted free. She hesitated, quickly looking between William and Edgar.

"Go now!" Edgar shouted, struggling with one of the men.

Alice fled down the corridor, her mother's Bible and her journal still clutched tightly to her chest, the sounds of the struggle fading behind her as darkness swallowed her whole.

Alice's heart hammered against her ribs as she plunged into the darkness. Behind her, the sounds of struggle faded into the night. William's desperate shout—"Run!"—echoed in her mind, propelling her forward even as fear threatened to freeze her limbs.

The grounds of Pullman Manor gave way to tangled undergrowth as Alice fled toward the woods. Branches clawed at her dress, tearing the fabric she'd mended so carefully over the years. The weight of her father's last gift, her mother's Bible, pressed against her chest.

She dared not look back. If William had been captured—

No. She couldn't think of that now.

The moon slipped behind clouds, plunging the forest into deeper darkness. Alice stumbled over a root, falling hard against the damp earth. Pain shot through her palm where a stone had cut it. For a moment, she lay there, breath coming in ragged gasps, the enormity of her situation threatening to overwhelm her.

"Get up," she whispered to herself, her father's voice seeming to echo the command in her mind. "Get up, Alice."

She pushed herself to her feet, catching her breath as best she could.

The distant shouts of Pullman's men searching the grounds spurred her deeper into the woods. Alice knew these paths from her childhood; her father had walked them with her countless times, pointing out wildflowers and discussing theology beneath these very trees. Now they offered shelter, concealing her from those who would silence her.

As the sounds of pursuit grew fainter, Alice slowed her pace. Her lungs burned with each breath, but something else burned brighter within her—resolve. She hadn't chosen this path, but now that she walked it, she would not falter.

Finding a small clearing bathed in moonlight, Alice sank down against the trunk of an ancient oak.

"No, no, no," she whispered, her voice breaking in the stillness of the forest.

She checked every page, every crease, even the binding itself, but found nothing. Edgar had rescued her journal from his father's office, but he couldn't have known about the papers. How could he? She'd never told anyone about them, not even William. She had just found them that evening.

Alice clutched the Bible to her chest, tears welling in her eyes. Her father's work, his sacrifice—all of it remained locked away in Pullman Manor, where it could no longer threaten Silas. The truth that had cost her father his life was once again buried, just as he had been.

A sob escaped her lips before she could stifle it. She had had the evidence in her hands. She'd carried it next to her heart. And now it was lost, perhaps forever.

"I'm sorry, Father," she whispered, leaning against the rough bark of the tree trunk. "I've failed you."

The weight of this loss pressed down on her more heavily than all her years at Pullman Manor combined. It wasn't just paper she had lost—it was her father's voice, his final act of courage, the justice he had died seeking.

Alice wiped her tears with the back of her hand, leaving a smudge of dirt across her cheek. Despite her gratitude for

Edgar's bravery in retrieving her journal, the absence of those papers left a hollow ache in her chest. Without them, what proof did she have? Who would believe the word of an orphaned girl against the powerful Silas Pullman?

WHAT COMES NEXT

Alice stumbled through the darkness, her breath forming small clouds in the night air. The woods had given way to open country hours ago, and now she traversed unfamiliar paths, guided only by William's hastily whispered directions. Her shoes, never meant for such a journey, had rubbed her heels raw. The Bible pressed against her chest beneath her shawl, it didn't feel any lighter, but Alice felt a painful ache whenever she thought of the papers that had been hidden within it until recently.

The bitter cold cut through her thin dress, numbing her fingers and toes. She'd been walking since around midnight, stopping only when exhaustion threatened to topple her. Now, as dawn approached, a small village emerged from the mist—Thornfield, it must be.

"Find Mrs Bennett," William had said. "The widow of Professor Bennett from Cambridge. Her cottage stands at the village edge with blue shutters and roses by the gate."

Alice's legs trembled as she approached the cottage. What if they'd followed her? What if Mrs Bennett turned her away? The thought of Grimsby's hands or an asylum cell made her shiver more violently than the cold.

She knocked softly, then louder when no answer came. The door creaked open, revealing a plump woman with kind eyes and silver-streaked hair.

"Mrs Bennett?" Alice's voice cracked.

"Yes, child. Goodness, you're frozen through!"

Alice swayed on her feet. "William Thornton sent me. I'm—"

"Come in before you catch your death," Mrs Bennett interrupted, pulling her inside.

The cottage enveloped Alice in warmth. A fire crackled in the hearth, casting dancing shadows on whitewashed walls. The scent of freshly baked bread mingled with herbs hanging from the ceiling beams. After Pullman Manor's oppressive grandeur, the simple comfort of this place brought tears to Alice's eyes.

Mrs Bennett wrapped a woollen blanket around Alice's shoulders and guided her to a chair by the fire. "Drink this," she said, pressing a steaming mug into Alice's hands.

The tea warmed Alice from within as Mrs Bennett busied herself preparing a plate of bread and preserves. For the first time in hours, Alice felt the rigid tension in her shoulders begin to ease.

Alice said quietly. "It might put you in danger."

Mrs Bennett's smile was gentle but knowing. "My dear, this cottage has sheltered many who needed a safe haven. Your secrets are your own to keep or share as you wish."

Alice sat in the chair by the fire, her hands trembling less now as warmth gradually returned to her limbs. The Bible and journal lay beside her.

She told Mrs Bennett everything—her father's death, the hidden documents, Grimsby's advances, the plan to commit her to an asylum. Words had tumbled out in a desperate rush, as though keeping them inside a moment longer might suffocate her.

Mrs Bennett listened without interruption, her face growing graver with each revelation. When Alice finally fell silent, the older woman reached across and took her hands.

"My dear child, what courage you've shown." Her grip was firm, reassuring. "William was right to send you to me."

"I've nowhere else to go," Alice whispered. "If Mr Pullman finds me—"

"He shan't find you here." Mrs Bennett's voice carried a surprising steel beneath its gentle tone. "This cottage has stood apart from prying eyes for many years, it was my father's before he passed it down to me, and I've sheltered others before you."

Alice glanced up, surprised. "Others?"

"My husband believed education should be available to all, regardless of station. Sometimes that meant providing sanctuary to those who shared that belief but found themselves... *inconvenient* to powerful men." A shadow crossed her face. "Silas Pullman is not the first man to value profit above human dignity."

Mrs Bennett rose and added another log to the fire. The flames leapt higher, casting her silhouette against the wall.

"You may stay as long as you need, Alice. This room will be yours." She gestured toward a small door off the sitting room. "No one will look for you here, and you'll have time to decide what to do, if anything at all."

For the first time since fleeing Pullman Manor, Alice felt the vice-like grip of fear loosen around her chest. She'd found not just shelter but understanding.

"Thank you," she managed, her voice barely audible.

Mrs Bennett smiled, the firelight softening the lines of her face. "Rest now. This afternoon is soon enough to face what comes next."

SANCTUARY

Alice settled into the small bed in Mrs Bennett's spare room, her hands still trembling slightly. Mrs Bennett had asked her if she wanted anything, and she only had one request: a journal and some ink. The unfamiliar leather binding of this new book still offered a strange comfort.

She dipped the nib of the borrowed pen into ink and began to write:

Dear Providence,

I find myself in yet another unfamiliar room, though this one feels more like a sanctuary than a prison. The walls don't press in with judgment, and for the first time in years, I need not whisper my prayers or hide these pages beneath a floorboard.

Alice paused, watching moonlight filter through the curtains. The weight of all that had transpired pressed upon her chest, demanding release through her pen.

. . .

Father once said that truth, like water, will always find its path forward, no matter the obstacles placed before it. I know his truth now —the knowledge of Mr Pullman's callous disregard for children's lives. Those poor broken bodies brought to the kitchen haunt my dreams. Mary Pemberton's face, so like the child I once comforted during her brother's illness, now bears scars that should never mark one so young. But with no way to prove anything.

Dear Providence, Through the loss of my father's meticulous documentation, justice might still not reach those who believed themselves beyond its grasp? What do I do with this vengeance that drives me? The Bible tells us that vengeance is yours so please help me. If only I had the papers now, and could do something with them to see justice realized.

Days melted into weeks, and weeks into months. Alice filled page after page, her writing growing stronger as her resolve solidified. The quiet cottage became both refuge and monastery —a place where Alice could finally hear her own thoughts clearly.

Three months have passed since I fled Pullman Manor. Three months without word of William. Does he think of me as I think of him? Our conversations beneath the oak tree sustain me still—the way his eyes lit up when discussing Milton, how carefully he considered my thoughts on theological matters when others would have dismissed them.

I miss him with an ache that surprises me in its persistence. Is this what Mother felt for Father? This certainty that one's soul has recognised its companion?

. . .

When loneliness threatened to overwhelm her, Alice would return to her journal, filling its pages with detailed plans for schools where factory children might learn, imagining curricula that would nurture minds broken by industrial cruelty.

Today I walked past the village school and watched children playing freely in the yard. What might Mary Pemberton have become if afforded such opportunity? What might any of them have become if their bodies weren't sacrificed to the machines?

Father believed one voice speaking truth could change hearts. I must believe this too, even as days stretch endlessly before me. Each word I write feels like practice for the day when I might finally speak aloud again.

WILLIAM'S FATE

William stood before the school board, their faces arranged in varying expressions of discomfort. The man at the head of the table, Mr Whitfield, wouldn't meet his eyes.

"I'm afraid we must terminate your position, Mr Thornton." The words hung in the stale air of the cramped office. "Recent... associations have made your continued employment untenable."

William's jaw tightened. "My associations?"

One of the board members cleared his throat. "Mr Pullman has expressed concerns about your judgment. He's been most generous to this institution."

"And his generosity comes with conditions," William said, his voice level despite the anger coursing through him. "Conditions that include dismissing anyone who questions his business practices."

"That's quite enough, Mr Thornton." Mr Whitfield finally looked up. "Your belongings must be cleared out by week's end."

Outside, William paused beneath a skeletal oak tree. Snow fell in delicate flurries, dusting his shoulders. Three months since he'd helped Alice escape, and Pullman's reach extended even here, two towns away. If Pullman could destroy his position so easily, what might he do to Alice if William led him to her?

The following fortnight saw William in London, standing before a modest brick building. The Progressive School for Boys wasn't grand—nothing like the position he'd lost—but its founder, Mr Jenkins, believed education should cultivate moral conscience alongside intellect.

"We can't offer much in terms of salary," Mr Jenkins said, showing William the cramped classroom where thirty boys from London's poorer districts would soon gather. "But we can offer freedom to teach as your conscience dictates."

"That's worth more than gold," William replied.

By day, William taught mathematics and literature. By night, he wrote feverishly by candlelight, his heartbreak now fuelling his articles on industrial reform.

His first publication in The Morning Chronicle drew modest attention. His second, detailing specific injuries sustained by child workers, prompted a letter from a parliamentarian named Howard Ellis.

"Your accounts align with what I've witnessed in Manchester," Ellis told William over tea in a modest café. "We need men like you—educated, articulate—to help us build support for the Factory Acts amendments."

William shrugged. "I'm just a schoolteacher."

"You're a voice for those who have none," Ellis countered. "And your connection to Reverend Wells gives your words authenticity that others lack."

William thought of Alice—her intelligence, her courage, her faith in justice. For her sake, he would keep his distance. For her father's sake, he would continue the fight.

"Very well," William said. "Tell me how I can help."

DISTANT MESSAGES

Alice sat by the window in Mrs Bennett's cottage, the morning light spilling across the small wooden table where she had spread the newspaper. Her fingers traced the columns of print until they settled on a particular notice in the personal advertisements:

To one who seeks Providence: In Matthew 5:6, comfort awaits. The path remains true though obscured by clouds.

Her breath caught. The reference to Providence—her journal's faithful addressee—could be no coincidence. *Matthew 5:6: Blessed are those who hunger and thirst for righteousness, for they shall be filled.* Their shared lesson on the Beatitudes beneath the oak tree at Pullman Manor had been particularly meaningful. William had spoken passionately about righteousness as not merely personal piety but social justice.

Alice pressed the newspaper to her chest, warmth spreading through her despite the morning chill. He had found a way to reach her.

The following week, Alice ventured into the village and paid for her own small notice: *The student recalls Psalm 27:14. Light persists even in darkness.*

Their coded correspondence continued this way—Scripture passages chosen not for their literal meaning but for the memories they evoked between them. Each verse represented a moment shared, a conversation had, a connection forged in those precious afternoons of learning.

That evening, Alice pulled out her journal, its leather binding worn smooth from constant handling. She dipped her pen and began to write:

Dear Providence—and William, wherever you may be tonight—

I found your message today. How clever you are, my friend, to speak so boldly yet so discreetly. The verse you chose brought me back to that autumn afternoon when you taught me that righteousness demands action, not merely contemplation.

Alice paused, watching the ink dry on the page. Her writing had evolved since those early desperate entries after her father's death. William's tutelage had given structure to her thoughts, but it was their separation that had imbued her words with new urgency and purpose.

I carry your teachings with me daily, she continued. *Not merely the lessons of grammar and composition, but of courage. When I feel most alone, I remember how you looked at me—truly saw me—when all others in that house wished me invisible.*

Each newspaper message became a lifeline, proof that somewhere William remained steadfast in his concern for her. Sometimes weeks passed between communications, but they always came—references to Job's perseverance, David's courage,

Esther's advocacy for her people.

WINTER SLUMBER

Alice found herself changing in subtle ways as winter yielded to spring. Mrs Bennett's cottage, once merely a sanctuary, had become a place of transformation. The older woman possessed a remarkable library filled with texts on philosophy, politics, and social reform that would have scandalized the Pullmans.

"You've a mind that deserves proper nourishment," Mrs Bennett had said, placing a worn copy of Mary Wollstonecraft's writings in Alice's hands. "Your father gave you roots. Now it's time to grow branches."

And grow she did. Alice's journal entries evolved from private reflections to articulated arguments. She drafted letters —some sent, others merely exercises—addressing the conditions she'd witnessed in Pullman's mill. Mrs Bennett introduced her to a circle of like-minded women who gathered fortnightly in the village to discuss reform.

"Miss Wells, your firsthand account would strengthen our petition considerably," said Mrs Fairchild, a sharp-eyed widow whose husband had been a factory inspector. "The authorities dismiss women's concerns as hysterical fancies, but we who listen know the truth when we hear it."

Alice hesitated, twisting her hands in her lap. "I've never spoken publicly."

"Neither had I, until necessity demanded it," Mrs Fairchild replied. "Courage isn't the absence of fear, but acting despite it."

The words echoed William's teachings. Alice nodded, determination replacing uncertainty.

In her room that evening, Alice unfolded William's latest coded message from the newspaper. The biblical reference spoke of standing firm in adversity. She traced the printed words with her fingertip, feeling his presence despite the miles between them.

"You taught me more than Latin and composition," she whispered. "You showed me that words can become actions."

She understood now that their connection transcended romantic attachment. They were partners in purpose, their separate paths somehow intertwined in service to the same cause. This knowledge sustained her through lonely nights when doubt crept in like the evening chill.

At her small writing desk, Alice organised her observations. Tomorrow she would meet with the reform committee. She would speak her truth—not merely for William or her father, but for Mary Pemberton and countless children like her.

Outside her window, crocuses pushed through the thawing earth—stubborn, resilient harbingers of change. Alice watched them sway in the breeze, their purple heads nodding as if in agreement with her thoughts. The world was awakening from its winter slumber, and so was she.

SOLIDARITY

Alice's heart hammered against her ribs as she stood before the reform committee. The parlour of Mrs Fairchild's home had been transformed into an impromptu assembly hall, with chairs arranged in neat rows facing a small table where Alice now stood. Afternoon light streamed through lace curtains, illuminating the faces of two dozen women who watched her with expectant eyes.

"I was fourteen when my father died," Alice began, her voice barely audible. She cleared her throat and tried again. "My father spoke against the conditions in the mill houses until his last breath."

"These are not merely statistics, they are people." Alice continued, her voice growing stronger. "Each number represents a child, like Mary Pemberton, who lost three fingers when machinery caught her sleeve. She was nine years old."

A murmur rippled through the assembly. Alice described the locked fire exits, the unguarded machinery, and the children working twelve hour shifts. She spoke of dust-filled lungs and stunted growth, of accidents concealed and inspectors deceived.

"I have seen these children carried from the rubble," Alice

said. "I have cleaned their wounds while men like Silas Pullman discussed how to hide the truth."

When she finished, the room fell silent. Then Mrs Bennett rose from her chair.

"What this young woman has endured to bring us this testimony deserves our utmost respect," she declared. "And our action."

One by one, the women stood. Some shared their own stories—of husbands injured, of children weakened by factory conditions. Others offered practical support—connections to sympathetic newspaper editors, access to parliamentary representatives.

Alice felt something unfamiliar bloom within her chest. For years at Pullman Manor, she had been invisible. Now these women—strangers until weeks ago—saw her, heard her, believed her.

"Your father would be proud," Mrs Fairchild said, squeezing Alice's hand. "As would Mr Thornton, I've no doubt."

At the mention of William, a bittersweet ache spread through Alice's chest. How she wished he could have witnessed this moment—her voice finally finding its strength, her father's work continuing through her. She wondered where William was now, whether his own efforts had met with success or setback.

FLAMES

Sarah winced as her loom clattered, the familiar rhythm punctuated by an ominous creaking from the beams overhead. Twelve years at Pullman's mill had taught her to read its sounds like a mother knows her child's cough. This sound was wrong.

"Did you hear that?" she whispered to Tom at the next machine.

Tom nodded without looking up. "Best not mention it. Jenkins got his wages docked last week for pointing out the crack in the support beam."

Sarah's gaze darted to the ceiling where water stains spread like bruises across the wooden beams. The spring rains had been heavy, and the roof leaked in a dozen places. Buckets dotted the floor, filling steadily while workers navigated around them.

"They've got to do something," Sarah muttered. "My Billy works upstairs, right under the worst of it."

"Mr Pullman was here yesterday," Tom replied. "Walked straight past the problem, he did. Only concerned about the production numbers."

Around them, the factory floor hummed with activity—children darting between machines, women hunched over looms, men hauling carts of raw cotton. Yet beneath the mechanical din ran an undercurrent of nervous whispers. Everyone had noticed the sagging beams, the widening cracks.

"Speed it up!" bellowed the foreman from the overseer's platform. "We're behind schedule!"

The engines roared louder, belts spinning faster. The entire building seemed to shudder.

Then it happened.

A tremendous crack split the air—louder than any machine—followed by a splintering groan of timber giving way. Sarah looked up as the ceiling collapsed in a shower of wood and slate. A massive support beam crashed down, crushing two looms mere yards away.

Then came the flames.

The lanterns shattered as they fell, oil splashing across cotton bales. Fire erupted in hungry orange tongues, racing along the floor and up the walls.

"Billy!" Sarah screamed, lunging toward the staircase that led to the upper floor.

Smoke billowed through the mill, thick and black, choking lungs and stinging eyes. Workers stampeded toward the main entrance, only to find it jammed with bodies all pushing at once.

"The side door!" someone shouted.

A group broke away, racing toward the exit by the loading bay. Sarah followed, desperate for any escape that might lead to the upper floor. They reached the door, hands clawing at the handle.

It wouldn't budge.

"It's locked!" a man cried, rattling the handle frantically. "They've locked the bloody door!"

"All of them are!" came another voice through the thickening smoke. "Pullman had them locked this morning—said too much cotton was going missing!"

Horrified understanding rippled through the crowd. They were trapped.

"My children!" wailed a woman, spinning wildly. "My babies are upstairs!"

Sarah pushed against the tide of bodies, fighting her way toward the stairs. The smoke was a living thing now, pressing down, filling every space. Through watering eyes, she saw other parents doing the same—crawling, climbing, screaming names into the roaring inferno.

"Billy!" she screamed again, voice breaking. "Billy, where are you?"

The flames answered, crackling as they devoured the mill that had devoured so many childhoods.

THE GARDENER'S SECRETS

Alice stood frozen by Mrs Bennett's cottage window, watching as another column of smoke spiralled from the direction of Pullman's mill, visible even miles away. For three days, the dark plume had hung over the village like a shroud. Whispers reached her through Mrs Bennett's visitors—mothers with hollow eyes, sisters with trembling hands.

"Twenty-seven dead, they're saying now." Mrs Fairchild's voice quivered as she accepted a cup of tea from Mrs Bennett. "And dozens more injured. Some with burns so severe the doctor doesn't expect them to last the week."

Alice's fingers curled around the windowsill. She recognised names among the dead—Samuel Atkins who'd once brought fish to her father when he was ill; little Betsy Wright whose mother had sewn Alice's confirmation dress; Tom Pemberton, Mary's younger brother.

"They're saying the doors were locked." Mrs Fairchild's words hung in the air. "Locked from the outside. To prevent theft, Pullman claims."

Alice's heart hammered against her ribs. Her father's notes burned in her mind—his detailed accounts of locked exits, his warnings ignored. She slipped away while the women continued their grim tally, retrieving her shawl from the hook by the door.

"I must go," she whispered to Mrs Bennett, who stood in the hallway with concern etched across her face. "Thomas might know more."

"Alice, it's too dangerous—"

"I'll stay hidden. The household will be in disarray with the fire. No one will notice me speaking with the gardener."

The walk to Pullman Manor stretched before her like a tightrope. Each step carried risk, but the pull of truth drove her forward. She kept to the hedgerows, ducking low when carriages passed.

Thomas was alone in the kitchen garden when she found him, his weathered hands moving mechanically among the vegetables. His face, when he turned at her approach, looked a decade older than when she'd last seen him.

"Miss Alice," he whispered, glancing nervously toward the house. "You shouldn't be here."

"The mill, Thomas. I had to know."

His hands trembled as he set down his trowel. "Worst thing I've seen in all my years. Bodies laid out in the churchyard, some burnt beyond recognition." His voice cracked. "I helped carry them. Little ones no bigger than sacks of flour."

Alice pressed her hand to her mouth.

"Sarah Wilkins crawled through fire trying to reach her boy. Found her with her arms still stretched out toward the stairs where he'd been working."

Thomas's eyes grew distant. "Just like your mother, all those years ago."

Alice froze. "My mother?"

"The first mill fire. Twenty years back, before you were born." Thomas wiped his eyes with a soil-stained handkerchief. "Your mother was there, working as a seamstress in the adjoining building. She tried to save three trapped children. Got them out, she did, but the burns..." He shook his head. "Never fully recovered. That's why your father fought so hard for those children. He couldn't save your mother, but he tried to save them."

Alice stared at Thomas, her mind struggling to absorb this revelation about her mother. All these years, she'd known only that her mother had died in childbirth. No one—not even her father—had ever mentioned a mill fire or her mother's heroism.

"There's more," Thomas said, glancing toward the house. "Wait here."

He disappeared behind the garden shed, returning moments later with a small tin box, its surface pitted with rust. "Your father gave me these for safekeeping after your mother passed. I don't know why he entrusted them to me. Perhaps God told him to, so that I would be here to give them to you, little one. You father said they were too painful to keep but too precious to destroy. I thought they were too heavy to give to you, with how precarious your position was, but now… I'm sorry it took me so long."

Alice's hands trembled as Thomas placed the box in her palms.

"Letters," he explained. "Between your parents. And notes your father kept about the mills. He buried himself in that work after your mother died—like he was trying to make amends for something that wasn't his fault."

Inside the box lay bundles of letters tied with faded ribbon. Alice untied the topmost bundle, unfolding a letter written in her father's familiar handwriting.

My dearest Eleanor,

I cannot forgive myself for not speaking out sooner. If I had challenged Pullman when your brother first reported the unsafe conditions, perhaps he and your father might still be with us. Their deaths in that machinery accident haunt my dreams. I have failed your family in the worst possible way.

Alice's breath caught. Her mother's family—her own blood relations—had died in Pullman's mill before she was born.

Another letter, this one from her mother:

Stephen,

You must not carry this burden. My father and brother knew the risks. What matters now is that you continue speaking truth against the powerful. Margaret understands—she promised to help when she marries Silas.

"Margaret?" Alice whispered, looking up at Thomas. "Mrs Pullman?"

Thomas nodded grimly. "Your father and Mrs Pullman were close cousins, grew up together. She promised to use her position to improve conditions once she married Silas. But wealth changes people. She chose comfort over conscience."

Alice sifted through more letters, finding one that made her heart ache:

Margaret has refused to help. Says Silas would never permit it. I hardly recognise the woman I once admired. She claims he practically demands her silence, but I call it cowardice. She has chosen wealth over righteousness, security over truth.

. . .

"All this time," Alice murmured, "she knew what her husband was doing. She knew about my family's suffering."

Alice clutched the letters to her chest, each page a piece of a puzzle she'd never known existed. The truth of her family's connection to Pullman burned like a coal in her mind. Her mother's bravery, her father's guilt, Margaret Pullman's betrayal—it formed a tapestry of suffering and silence that spanned decades.

"I must go," she whispered to Thomas. "But thank you for this. For keeping these safe all these years."

Thomas nodded, his weathered face solemn. "Your father was a good man, Miss Alice. The best I've known. And your mother—she had fire in her soul. I see it in you too."

Alice carefully replaced the letters in the tin box, tucking it beneath her shawl. As she turned to leave, Thomas touched her arm.

"There's talk," he said, his voice dropping lower, "that Edgar's been hurt. He was at the mill when it happened. Tried to help the children escape."

Alice's heart constricted. Edgar, despite his upbringing, had become a hero.

"How badly?"

"Burns to his hands and face. He's in the hospital. They say he keeps asking for you."

Alice hesitated, torn between safety and compassion. "I can't, Thomas. If they find me here—"

"I understand." He pressed something into her palm—a small pouch of forget-me-not seeds. "Remember what I told you. They survive the harshest winters."

With a final nod, Alice slipped away through the kitchen garden, the tin box of letters heavy against her side. Each step took her further from Pullman Manor, but the revelations followed her like shadows.

Back at Mrs Bennett's cottage, Alice sat alone in her room,

spreading the letters across the bed. Her father's anguish, her mother's courage, Margaret's betrayal—all of it formed a constellation of truth she could no longer ignore.

She opened her journal and began to write, her pen moving with newfound purpose.

Dear Providence,

Today I learned that my battle with the Pullmans began long before my birth. My mother died not just from childbirth but from injuries sustained saving children from Pullman's negligence. My father's crusade was not merely righteous indignation but a husband's grief seeking justice.

The fire has claimed more innocent lives, just as my father feared it would. But this time, I will not be silenced. I will not look away. For my father, for my mother, for Mary Pemberton and all the children who deserve better—I will speak the truth, whatever the cost.

HEADLINES

Alice folded the latest newspaper with trembling hands. Twenty-seven souls lost to flames and smoke. Twenty-seven families shattered. Names filled the columns—fathers, mothers, children as young as eight—all sacrificed to Pullman's greed. The paper detailed how rescuers had found bodies piled against locked doors, fingernails broken from desperate attempts to escape.

She closed her eyes, but the images remained. Mary Pemberton's younger brother among the dead. Three generations of the Finch family gone in a single night. The Coopers' daughter, who'd just turned twelve last week.

"They're saying it wasn't an accident," Mrs Bennett said softly, placing a cup of tea beside Alice. "Inspector's report mentions the locked doors specifically."

"It wasn't." Alice's voice hardened. "Pullman ordered those doors locked to prevent workers from stealing cotton scraps. Pennies saved at the cost of lives."

Through the window, Alice watched families in black moving through the village like shadows. Their grief hung in the air, palpable as the smoke that still rose from the mill's skeleton. Workers who'd survived gathered in small groups, their faces masks of terror and disbelief. She recognised in them the same haunted expressions her father had described after visiting injured parishioners.

"They're saying Silas might face criminal charges," Mrs Bennett continued. "Though his solicitors are already working to shield him."

Alice's laugh held no humour. "Men like Pullman rarely face true consequences. Their money builds walls between themselves and justice."

She thought of her father's notes, the letters, the years of documented negligence. Evidence that should damn Pullman ten times over. Yet doubt gnawed at her. How many inspectors had been bribed before? How many magistrates dined at Pullman's table?

That evening, Alice wrote in her journal by candlelight, her pen scratching across the page with renewed purpose.

The mill stands as a monument to greed now—a graveyard where dreams and futures lie buried beneath charred timber. I think of Mary, of all those children whose voices have been silenced. Who will speak for them if not those of us who remain?

Father believed words could change hearts. He believed truth, spoken boldly, could overcome even the most entrenched power. Was he naive? Or braver than I can comprehend?

Alice paused, watching shadows dance across the wall. Her father had died pursuing justice. Her mother had perished saving children from similar flames. Their blood ran in her veins.

. . .

I will not allow their sacrifices to be forgotten. These papers, these testimonies—they are not just evidence. They are voices crying out from beyond the grave. I must ensure they are heard.

She dipped her pen again, writing with the steady hand of newfound resolve.

The time for silence has passed. Father's work remains unfinished, but I am his daughter. His courage is my inheritance. Whatever comes, I will stand for truth.

LONDON

William stood before the gathering at Ellsworth Hall, his collar tight against his throat as the weight of his words hung in the smoke-filled air. Faces peered up at him through the haze—labourers with calloused hands, reformists with furrowed brows, and a handful of parliamentarians whose quills scratched against parchment.

William straightened his posture as he addressed the packed assembly room. The faces before him—some hopeful, others skeptical—reminded him of all he'd witnessed in Yorkshire. His throat tightened at the memory of all those children's haunted eyes.

"Gentlemen, I speak not from hearsay but from direct observation," William began, his voice steady despite the emotion swelling in his chest. "The conditions in our nation's mills and workhouses are not merely unpleasant—they are deadly."

He unfolded several papers containing his meticulously compiled notes.

"Children as young as six work twelve-hour days among machinery with no guards or safety measures. Their small fingers are considered expendable tools, perfect for reaching into moving parts where adults cannot." William paused as murmurs rippled through the crowd. "I have personally tended to a child whose arm was mangled beyond recognition when exhaustion caused her to slip."

William's gaze swept across the room, lingering on the factory owners who shifted uncomfortably in their chairs.

"The air in these establishments is thick with cotton dust and chemical fumes. Women collapse daily from the heat and lack of ventilation. Men who dare speak of these conditions find themselves without work the following day."

William's voice grew more passionate. "We speak of Britain as civilised, yet we permit practices that would shame the most barbaric society. These are not unfortunate accidents but calculated risks taken by those who view their workers as machinery rather than human beings."

The room had fallen completely silent.

"When a child's fingers are crushed, it is recorded as 'mechanical wastage.' When a mother suffocates on cotton dust, it is noted as 'natural causes.'" William's green eyes flashed with controlled anger. "I ask you, gentlemen—at what point does negligence become murder?"

A murmur rippled through the crowd. William caught sight of Howard Ellis, MP [Member of Parliament], leaning forward in his chair.

The room fell silent. William thought of Alice, of her courage.

"Gentlemen, we stand at a crossroads. Will we continue to build our prosperity upon the broken bodies of children? Or will we ensure no more families are destroyed by unchecked greed?"

Several men shifted uncomfortably in their seats. A factory owner near the front adjusted his cravat, his face flushed with indignation.

"This is radical nonsense," he hissed to his companion. "Who is this upstart schoolmaster?"

William met his gaze without flinching. "I am merely the voice of those who cannot speak for themselves."

Three days later, William stood before Headmaster Jenkins, watching as the older man's fingers drummed against a letter bearing the Pullman seal.

"The board has reached a unanimous decision," Jenkins said, unable to meet William's eyes. "Your position here is no longer tenable."

William nodded, his throat tight. "Because I spoke the truth?"

"Because you've made powerful enemies, Mr Thornton. The school cannot afford such associations."

William gathered his few belongings from the small desk where he'd marked essays late into the night. The faces of his students flashed before him—bright, curious minds he would no longer guide.

Yet as he stepped into the grey London afternoon, a strange lightness filled his chest. He had chosen truth over security, just as Alice had. Just as Reverend Wells had before them both.

~

William folded the newspaper with trembling hands, the bold headline searing into his consciousness: "FACTORY INFERNO CLAIMS 27 LIVES—PULLMAN MILL DOORS FOUND LOCKED." The crowded London coffeehouse continued its hum of conversation around him, but William had gone deaf to it all. His eyes scanned the article again, searching for names he recognised among the dead and injured.

"Edgar Pullman, son of mill owner Silas Pullman, sustained severe burns while attempting to rescue trapped workers," the article stated. William's chest tightened. Edgar had chosen courage in the end, just as he'd done the night of Alice's escape.

A smaller article on the following page announced the forthcoming trial of Silas Pullman on charges of criminal negligence. William's heartbeat quickened. After years of impunity, the man might finally face justice for his callous disregard for human life.

William folded the newspaper and set it aside, a bitter taste filling his mouth. The headline promised justice, but experience had taught him better. Men like Silas Pullman weren't held to the same standards as common folk.

"Criminal negligence," he muttered, drawing a skeptical glance from the gentleman at the neighbouring table. "As if he'll ever see the inside of a courtroom."

William signalled for more tea, though what he truly wanted was something stronger. The trial would drag on for months, perhaps years. Pullman would hire the finest barristers in England, men who knew how to twist the law into whatever shape best served their client's interests. Evidence would mysteriously disappear. Witnesses would suddenly develop faulty memories or find themselves unable to attend proceedings.

Twenty-seven souls lost, and for what? A few extra pounds in Pullman's already overflowing coffers. The thought of Mary Pemberton's brother among the dead made William's stomach clench. How many families had Pullman destroyed with his greed?

William pulled out his pocket watch—the one luxury he'd allowed himself after receiving payment for his articles. Nearly three o'clock. He should be preparing for tomorrow's meeting with Howard Ellis and the parliamentary committee, but his mind refused to focus on anything beyond the newspaper's grim report.

"Justice delayed is justice denied," William whispered to himself, recalling one of Reverend Wells' favourite sayings he had learnt from Alice. The wheels of justice turned slowly for the common man, but for the wealthy, they scarcely moved at all. Pullman would use every connection, every favour owed, every pound in his possession to ensure he never faced consequences for those locked doors.

William wondered if Alice had seen the news yet. The thought of her reading about Edgar's injuries alone pained him. Despite everything, she'd always maintained that there was goodness in the boy. It seemed she'd been right.

William left a coin on the table and stepped into the damp London street. A decision crystallised in his mind with sudden clarity. He must return to Yorkshire immediately.

That evening, William packed his meagre belongings and wrote a brief note to Howard Ellis explaining his departure. The parliamentary committee would have to continue its work without him for now. Some matters transcended even the important work of reform.

As the train pulled away from London the following morning, William pressed his forehead against the cool glass of the window. The rhythmic clacking of wheels against tracks matched the anxious beating of his heart. A year had passed since he'd last seen Alice—a year of coded messages in newspaper columns, a year of wondering if she was safe, a year of carrying her image in his mind's eye.

The countryside rolled past, transforming from London's industrial sprawl to green fields dotted with sheep. William closed his eyes, remembering their last meeting, alone, in the churchyard—her face illuminated by moonlight, the weight of her mother's Bible in her hands, the touch of his lips against her forehead. He had promised to find a way for them to be together.

William opened the leather satchel on his lap and withdrew a small, worn volume of poetry they had once discussed beneath the oak tree. He had carried it with him through all his travels, a tangible connection to the woman whose intellect and courage had transformed him.

"I'm coming, Alice," he whispered to the passing landscape. "I'm coming home."

REUNION

Alice stood in Mrs Bennett's garden, her fingers absently tracing the velvet edge of a foxglove bloom. The evening light softened everything—the stone cottage, the weathered fence, the distant hills—casting the world in gentle amber hues. She had come outside to collect herbs for supper, but found herself lingering, watching the sunset paint the Yorkshire sky in strokes of pink and gold.

A movement at the garden gate caught her eye.

Alice's heart stumbled in her chest. There, silhouetted against the twilight, stood William.

Time seemed to crystallise around them. Neither moved. William appeared somehow both familiar and changed—his face leaner, his shoulders broader beneath his travel-worn coat. A small scar now marked his left cheek, and his eyes held shadows she hadn't seen before. Yet they were the same eyes that had first truly seen her, that had recognised her mind when others saw only her station.

For an endless moment, they simply looked at each other across Mrs Bennett's garden, drinking in the sight as parched souls might drink water.

Then something broke within Alice. Propriety, caution, restraint—all vanished like morning mist. She ran to him, her skirts catching on the lavender bushes, her feet barely touching the ground. William stepped forward and caught her in his arms, lifting her slightly as they collided.

The embrace closed a year of separation in an instant. Alice buried her face against his neck, breathing in the scent of him—wool and ink and something distinctly William. His arms tightened around her waist, solid and real and present after months of dreams and newspaper messages.

In that moment, the world beyond the garden fence ceased to exist. There was only this—his heartbeat against hers, his breath warming her hair, the slight tremble in his hands as they pressed against her back. Their embrace spoke volumes that words could never adequately express—the fear of loss, the weight of waiting, the quiet, steady love that had sustained them both through separation.

When William finally drew back enough to look at her face, his fingers gently traced her cheek. Alice saw his expression shift as he noted the shadows beneath her eyes, the new hollowness in her cheeks, the weariness etched into her features.

Alice struggled to find words as William's gaze held hers. His face bore new lines of weariness, and the scar on his cheek spoke of hardships she knew nothing about. Yet his eyes remained unchanged—kind, intelligent, seeing her completely.

"You're here," she whispered, her voice catching. "I feared—"

"I came as soon as I read about the fire," William said, his hands still resting lightly on her shoulders as though afraid she might vanish. "Edgar—is he—?"

"Recovering," Alice said. "He saved three children before the beam fell."

Mrs Bennett appeared at the cottage door, her silhouette framed by warm lamplight. She nodded once at William, then discreetly withdrew inside, leaving them their moment of reunion.

William guided Alice to the stone bench beneath the apple tree. As they sat, their shoulders touching, Alice felt the weight of the year's separation lifting. The evening breeze carried the scent of Mrs Bennett's roses, mingling with the distant smell of smoke that still hung over the valley.

"I lost my position," William said quietly. "Speaking out about the workhouses and mills cost me the school, but I had found work in London with reformers who care about what's happening here."

Alice's hand found his, their fingers intertwining with the ease of long familiarity. "And I found my voice," she said. "I've been speaking to committees, women who've lost children in the mills are coming forward with their stories."

William's thumb traced circles on the back of her hand. "I knew you would. Your father would be proud."

"I still write to Providence every night," Alice admitted, glancing up at him. "Though now I write with purpose rather than just to ease my heart."

William reached into his coat and withdrew a small, worn volume of poetry. "I carried this with me," he said. "The page you marked—about faith being the bird that feels the light when dawn is still dark."

Alice leaned her head against his shoulder, closing her eyes briefly. The days to come would bring challenges—Pullman's trial, the uncertain future of the mill workers, the path forward for them both. But tonight, in this garden where forget-me-nots bloomed along the fence, William had returned to her, and that was enough.

PLEDGE

Alice sat in Mrs Bennett's parlour, her fingers tracing the warmth of the teacup in her hands. The fire crackled and popped in the hearth, casting dancing shadows across the worn but polished furniture. How different this room felt from the cold grandeur of Pullman Manor—here, every cushion invited rest, every corner held books rather than ornaments meant only to impress.

William sat across from her in a high-backed chair, his face illuminated by the firelight. Between them, Mrs Bennett worked on her embroidery, her presence both comforting and proper. The older woman's occasional glances held approval rather than judgment, her needle moving steadily through the fabric.

"More tea, Mr Thornton?" Mrs Bennett asked, setting aside her needlework.

"No, thank you," William replied, his voice carrying a slight tremor that caught Alice's attention.

He rose from his chair and crossed to kneel before Alice. Her breath caught as he reached into his waistcoat pocket and withdrew something small that gleamed in the firelight.

"Alice," he began, his voice steadying as he spoke her name. "I came back not only for justice, but for you."

In his palm lay a simple gold band with a single modest pearl. The firelight caught its surface, sending warm reflections across his face.

"This was my mother's," William said. "She gave it to me before she passed, saying it should go to a woman of true heart and clear mind."

Alice felt tears prickling behind her eyes as William took her hand in his.

"I have nothing of wealth or station to offer," he continued, his gaze unwavering, "only a life of purpose beside me. Before, I asked you to wait a year, and now a year has passed. I am not where I thought I'd be, or where I'd want to be so I can provide for you... But I cannot wait any longer."

The simplicity of his words struck Alice more deeply than any elaborate declaration could have. In them, she heard not just love, but respect—for her mind, her principles, her very self.

"Alice Wells," William's cheek started to go rosy. "Will you marry me?"

"Yes," Alice whispered, a tear of joy falling down her cheek. "Yes, William."

As he slipped the ring onto her finger, Alice felt its weight—not just of the metal, but of all it represented. This was no mere ornament but a pledge between equals, a commitment to stand together against whatever came.

Mrs Bennett dabbed discreetly at her eyes with her handkerchief.

"The Pullmans won't make this simple," Alice said softly, looking down at the ring that now encircled her finger. "There will be consequences."

"I know," William replied, rising to sit beside her. "But we'll face them together."

"We cannot simply begin our life together while Silas

Pullman continues his corruption," Alice said, her voice soft but resolute. "Not when twenty-seven souls cry out from their graves."

William nodded, his hand still clasping hers. "I've heard whispers about a trial, but Silas has friends in high places. Money speaks louder than justice in these matters."

"Then we must make truth speak louder still." Alice straightened her shoulders, the same determination that had carried her through years at Pullman Manor rising within her chest.

William moved closer, their shoulders touching as they faced the fire. "Edgar might help us. His injury while saving those children has changed him. He's seen the consequences of his father's greed firsthand."

"And there's Thomas," Alice added, thinking of the old gardener. "He knew about my mother, kept letters all these years. He might know other secrets—other witnesses."

The firelight cast long shadows as they leaned toward each other, voices dropping to whispers as they began to outline their plan. Alice felt a curious blend of fear and certainty—the path ahead was fraught with danger, yet clearer than any she'd walked before.

"We must face the Pullmans once more," Alice said. The thought no longer filled her with dread. With William beside her, she could confront even Silas himself. "Silas has my father's notes. Alongside Edgar and Thomas as witnesses, that will be enough to put Silas behind bars, I'm sure of it."

Their fingers interlaced, a physical manifestation of their shared purpose. No words were needed for this silent pledge—to stand together, to fight for justice, to honor those who had suffered. In that moment, Alice understood that their love was not merely a private joy but a source of strength that could withstand whatever trials lay ahead.

CORNERED

Alice's heart pounded in her chest as she and William approached Pullman Manor. The imposing structure, once a symbol of wealth and power, now stood in disarray. Windows gaped like empty eye sockets, curtains billowing in the breeze where servants had left them undrawn. The gravel drive, usually meticulously raked, lay scattered with fallen leaves.

"It seems all the staff has left," William murmured, his hand steady on her elbow.

Alice nodded, her throat tight. "Margaret must have gone to her sister's in York. Lavinia would have fled to her fiancé's estate."

They climbed the steps to the front entrance. The heavy oak door, typically guarded by a footman, stood ajar. Alice pushed it open, wincing at the familiar creak that had once signalled her return from secret meetings with William.

"We need to find Father's notes," she whispered as they stepped into the cavernous entry hall. "The last time I saw them, Silas was putting them into a drawer in his desk."

William squeezed her hand. "Are you certain you wish to face him?"

Alice touched the simple pearl ring on her finger. "I've been invisible in this house for years. No more."

They moved cautiously through dimly lit hallways, past the drawing room where Lavinia had mocked her, past the library where she and William had first connected through hidden notes. The familiar corridors felt different now—less intimidating, more hollow.

Light spilled from beneath the study door. Alice exchanged a glance with William before pushing it open.

Silas Pullman sat alone at his massive desk, hair disheveled, waistcoat unbuttoned. Papers lay scattered before him, and a half-empty decanter of brandy stood at his elbow. He looked up, eyes narrowing as he recognised them.

"The charity case returns," he said, voice rough. "With her tutor in tow."

Alice stepped forward, chin raised. "I've come for my father's notes, Mr Pullman."

Silas's lip curled. "Your father—always the righteous one. His cousin Margaret wept for days after choosing me over him. Did you know that?"

The revelation struck Alice like a physical blow, but she kept her face impassive.

"Twenty-seven people died because you locked those doors," William said, moving to stand beside Alice.

Something shifted in Silas's eyes—calculation giving way to desperation. He glanced at the papers before him, then at the fireplace where flames licked at fresh logs.

"You have no proof," he snarled, suddenly lunging across the desk. He swept an armful of documents toward the fire, flinging them into the flames.

"No!" Alice cried, rushing forward.

The papers caught immediately, flames leaping higher as

Silas grabbed more documents from a drawer. In his haste, he knocked over the brandy decanter. Liquid splashed across the desk and floor, igniting as it touched the fireplace. Fire raced across the surface, consuming everything in its path.

"What have you done?" William shouted as smoke billowed upward, flames crawling rapidly up the heavy velvet curtains.

Heat seared Alice's face as she backed away, watching in horror as the study became engulfed. Silas stood frozen, surrounded by his own destruction, as the flames climbed higher around them.

The flames spread with horrifying speed. Alice barely had time to register the danger before William's arm shot out, pulling her backward as a burning timber crashed down where she'd stood seconds before. The roar of the fire drowned her startled cry as William shielded her body with his own, his shoulders hunched protectively over her.

"We need to get out," he shouted above the crackling inferno.

Alice nodded, but as they turned toward the door, another beam gave way with a sickening crack. William shoved her aside, taking the brunt of the impact as smoldering wood struck his shoulder and side. He crumpled to one knee with a strangled groan.

"William!" Alice dropped beside him, terror clawing at her throat. His face had gone white with pain, his breathing shallow.

For a heartbeat, her father's face superimposed over William's—pale, struggling for breath as pneumonia claimed him. The same helplessness threatened to overwhelm her, the same desperate prayer forming on her lips: *Not him too. Please, not him too.*

But William was still alive, still breathing. Still fighting.

"I'm all right," he managed, though his grimace belied his words. "We must go—now."

The smoke thickened around them, stinging Alice's eyes and

burning her lungs. She looped William's arm over her shoulders, supporting his weight as he struggled to stand. His body felt impossibly heavy against hers, but she refused to buckle.

"This way," she urged, half-dragging him toward the door as flames licked at the walls and ceiling.

The main corridor was already impassable, a wall of fire blocking their escape. William swayed against her, his consciousness fading.

"Alice," he mumbled, "leave me...get yourself out..."

"Never," she snapped, tightening her grip on his waist.

Mary Pemberton's voice echoed suddenly in her mind: "We'd escape through the servants' stairs when the foreman came round—there's passages all through these old houses that the masters never knew about."

"The servants' passage," Alice whispered, her eyes widening with hope. "William, there's another way."

She changed direction, guiding his stumbling steps toward the small door nearly hidden in the wood paneling. It led to narrow corridors where servants could move unseen between rooms—corridors she'd used countless times while carrying trays and linens.

"Just a little further," she encouraged, feeling William's weight grow heavier against her shoulder. The smoke swirled thicker around them, but Alice pressed forward, each laboured step bringing them closer to safety.

BEGGING FOR FORGIVENESS

Alice's lungs burned with each smoke-filled breath as she half-carried William through the narrow servants' passage. The heat pressed against them from all sides, but she could see the faint outline of a door ahead—their escape route to the kitchen yard.

"Almost there," she gasped, adjusting William's weight against her shoulder.

Then she heard it—a desperate cry cutting through the roar of the flames. Silas Pullman's voice, calling for help.

Alice froze, her heart hammering against her ribs. Part of her wanted to continue forward, to leave behind the man who had caused so much suffering. He had threatened to lock her away, had worked children to exhaustion, had perhaps even sent her father to his death.

Yet something else stirred within her—her father's voice, gentle but firm: "True charity means helping those who deserve it least."

"Did you hear that?" William murmured, his voice stronger now as consciousness fully returned.

Alice nodded, her throat tight. "It's Mr Pullman."

Their eyes met in the smoky half-light, understanding passing between them without words. William straightened slightly, grimacing through his pain.

"We can't leave him," Alice whispered, the decision settling in her chest like a stone.

William nodded. "No. We can't."

Together they turned back, following the desperate cries until they found Silas trapped beneath a fallen beam, flames creeping ever closer. His face, usually so composed and cruel, was contorted with terror and pain.

"Help me," he pleaded, all pretence of dignity abandoned.

Alice knelt beside him, assessing the beam. It was heavy but not impossible if they worked together. She met William's gaze, and he nodded again, bracing himself against the pain in his shoulder.

"On three," she said, positioning her hands beneath the smouldering wood.

Their combined strength barely shifted the beam at first, but Alice refused to yield. Sweat mingled with soot on her face as she strained, thinking of Mary Pemberton, of the locked doors, of her father's last fevered breaths—and still she pushed harder, feeling the weight begin to give.

"I'm sorry," Silas suddenly sobbed as they worked. "God help me, I'm sorry. Your father—he was right about everything. I knew the mill wasn't safe. I knew and I did nothing."

The beam moved enough for Silas to drag himself free. He collapsed at their feet, weeping openly now.

"I sent him to the Finch boy that night. I knew the river was rising. I wanted him gone, silenced—" His voice broke. "And now you save me. Why would you save me?"

Alice felt something release inside her chest—not forgiveness exactly, but the loosening of a knot that had bound her spirit since her father's death.

"Because it's what he would have done," she answered simply.

William helped Silas to his feet, and together the three of them stumbled toward the exit. Each step was laboured, the manor groaning and splintering around them as fire consumed the structure that had stood for generations.

They burst through the kitchen door into the cool night air just as a thunderous crash announced the collapse of the main staircase. Alice gulped fresh air into her burning lungs, William's arm still around her waist, Silas kneeling on the gravel beside them.

Behind them, Pullman Manor—once a symbol of oppression and fear—blazed against the night sky. Alice watched the flames consume the place that had imprisoned her spirit, feeling not triumph but a strange, cleansing relief.

Alice's chest heaved as she drew in lungfuls of sweet night air, each breath a gift after the choking smoke. William's arm encircled her waist, his body warm against hers, both of them leaning on each other for support. The heat from the burning manor pressed against their backs while the cool Yorkshire night air caressed their faces—a stark division between death and life.

Beside them, Silas collapsed to his knees on the gravel drive. His fine clothes were now tattered and singed, his face blackened with soot. All traces of the imperious mill owner had vanished, leaving only a broken man.

"God forgive me," he moaned, pressing his palms together in desperate supplication. "Forgive me for the children, for the locked doors, for Wells—"

Alice watched him, this man who had tormented her, threatened her, perhaps even caused her father's death. Yet she felt no triumph in his suffering. Instead, a curious emptiness filled the space where her hatred had lived.

"Please," Silas continued, rocking back and forth. "I've been blind. So blind. The money—it was never worth their lives."

William's fingers tightened around Alice's waist. She glanced up to find his green eyes fixed on her face, searching, questioning. Did he wonder if she could truly witness this without satisfaction? She wasn't entirely certain herself.

"Twenty-seven souls," Silas sobbed. "Twenty-seven souls on my conscience. And so many more... And your father—a good man who only wanted justice."

Alice trembled, not from cold but from the weight of the moment. Her father had taught her that true faith meant extending mercy even when it wasn't deserved. Standing here now, watching her enemy stripped of all bombast and bravado, she understood the profound difficulty of that teaching.

William's hand found hers, his thumb tracing gentle circles against her palm. They stood together, supporting each other as the man who had caused so much suffering begged God for the forgiveness he had never offered others.

JUSTICE

Alice sat in the crowded courtroom, her shoulders squared despite the weight of all that had happened. People had expected the trial to last for weeks, for Silas to hire the best lawyer he could and battle the charges however possible, but that was not the way things went.,

Alice watched as Silas stood before the judge, a diminished figure compared to the man who had once towered over her life.

"I plead guilty to all charges," he said, his voice carrying clearly through the hushed room. "The deaths at my mill were not accidents but the result of my negligence and greed."

A murmur rippled through the gallery. Alice felt William's hand close over hers, warm and steady.

"I cannot bring back those who died," Silas continued, "but I will spend what remains of my life making amends. Every penny of compensation ordered by this court will be paid in full."

The judge's sentencing was severe but just. Families of the victims would receive substantial compensation, and Silas would serve time for his crimes. As the gavel fell, Alice felt neither triumph nor vengeance—only a quiet certainty that truth had finally prevailed.

Both Silas Pullman and Mr Grimsby were sentenced to long sentences.

Outside the courthouse, Edgar approached them. His arm remained in a sling, a reminder of his bravery during the fire. The bandages on his face had been removed, revealing scars that would never fully heal.

"I've decided to renounce my inheritance," he told them, his voice steady despite the enormity of his decision. "I'll use what education I have to work for industrial reform."

"Your father would be proud," Alice said softly.

Edgar awkwardly adjusted his sling. "I'm not so sure."

"He has a long way to go, but your father has seen righteousness, Edgar." Alice smiled gently.

Edgar nodded, his eyes bright with unshed tears. "Lavinia and Lord Harrington have left for the continent. I doubt they'll return while the scandal remains fresh."

Alice thought of Lavinia, who had once mocked her as "the charity case." How strange that it was Lavinia who had fled, while Alice remained to see justice done.

"What will you do now?" Edgar asked.

Alice glanced at William, drawing strength from his presence. "We'll continue what my father started," she said simply. She looked down at the ring on her finger, "I've also got a wedding to attend."

A KNOCK AT THE DOOR

Alice smoothed the simple white dress she'd chosen for her wedding day. It wasn't grand like Lavinia's would have been, but it felt right—honest and true, like the life she hoped to build with William. Mrs Bennett had helped with the alterations, taking in the seams of a dress that had once belonged to her own daughter.

"A knock at the door, dear," Mrs Bennett called from downstairs.

Alice wasn't expecting anyone. Most of the preparations were complete for tomorrow's ceremony at her father's former parish church. She made her way down the narrow staircase, wondering who might be calling at this hour.

The door opened to reveal Margaret Pullman.

Alice froze, her hand instinctively tightening on the banister. Mrs Pullman stood alone, without the finery that had once marked her station. Her face seemed older, lined with experiences Alice couldn't begin to imagine.

"May I come in?" Margaret asked, her voice softer than Alice had ever heard it.

Mrs Bennett glanced at Alice, who nodded slowly.

They sat in Mrs Bennett's modest parlour, the silence stretching between them until Margaret finally spoke.

"I've come to ask your forgiveness, Alice," she said, her hands clasped tightly in her lap. "I failed you. I failed your father. And long before that, I failed your mother."

Alice remained silent, uncertain what to say to this woman who had watched her suffer in silence for years.

"Silas ordered all traces of your mother destroyed after your father's... after he died," Margaret continued. "He couldn't bear the reminders of what he'd done. But I couldn't—" Her voice broke. "I couldn't let everything of her disappear."

She reached into her bag and withdrew a small package wrapped in silk.

"These belonged to Eleanor. Your mother."

With trembling fingers, Alice unwrapped the silk. Inside lay a delicate gold wedding ring and a miniature portrait in an oval frame. She gasped as she looked upon her mother's face for the first time. The resemblance was unmistakable—the same eyes, the same curve of the mouth.

"You look just like her," Margaret whispered. "Every time I saw you, I saw her. Perhaps that's why I couldn't..."

Alice traced her finger over the miniature, feeling a connection to her mother that had always been told through others' memories, never her own eyes.

"Thank you," Alice said quietly, surprising herself with the sincerity in her voice.

PAST TO FUTURE

Alice stood in the vestibule of her father's former parish church, the same place where Reverend Stephen Wells had once delivered sermons that changed hearts and lives. Sunlight streamed through the stained glass windows, casting jewel-toned patterns across the worn stone floor. In her hands, she held her mother's wedding ring—so small and delicate, yet weighted with a history she was only beginning to understand.

"It's time," Mrs Bennett whispered, adjusting the simple wreath of wildflowers in Alice's hair.

Alice nodded, her heart fluttering beneath the modest white dress. She had no father to walk her down the aisle, but she felt his presence nonetheless, as surely as if he stood beside her.

The small congregation rose as Alice entered. The church wasn't filled with society's elite as it would have been for Lavinia's wedding, but with people whose lives had been woven into the fabric of Alice's own. Factory workers with scarred hands and unbowed spirits. Mrs Reynolds, who had slipped extra food onto Alice's plate when no one was looking. Thomas Buckley, standing tall despite his age, his weathered face creased with pride.

And there, at the back, sat Margaret Pullman, her eyes downcast, hands folded in her lap. Alice caught her gaze briefly, offering a small nod of acknowledgment.

At the altar waited William, his face alight with a joy that made Alice's heart swell. Beside him stood Edgar Pullman—though he had begun introducing himself simply as Edgar now, distancing himself from the family name and the legacy it carried.

William took Alice's hands in his as she reached him. "You look beautiful," he whispered.

"I brought my mother with me," Alice murmured, as she looked at their wedding rings. Her mother's sat there waiting for her. "And my father is here too, in every stone of this church."

The vicar began the ceremony, his voice filling the space where Reverend Wells had once stood. When the moment came to exchange rings, Alice's fingers trembled as William slipped her mother's gold band onto her finger. It fit perfectly, as if it had always been waiting for this moment.

"With this ring, I thee wed," William said, his voice steady and sure.

Alice looked down at the golden circle that had once symbolised her mother's love, now binding her to William. A circle unbroken, connecting past to future.

YOUR OWN STORIES

Alice stood at the front of the small classroom, watching sunlight filter through the tall windows of what had once been a wool merchant's storehouse. Now, six months after her wedding to William, the space had been transformed into something miraculous—a school for children who had never before been offered education.

"Today," she said, placing her hand on a stack of blank journals, "we begin something special."

Twenty faces looked back at her—some scarred, some thin, all bearing the unmistakable marks of mill work. Mary Pemberton sat in the front row, her maimed hand resting on the desk. Mary was to assist Alice. Alice had been tutoring Mary for months. Beside her was Billy Watson, whose father had died in the fire. At the back, three sisters who had been orphaned when both parents perished beneath collapsed machinery.

"These are your very own books," Alice continued, beginning to distribute the journals. "Not for sums or copying. These are for your thoughts, your stories, your truth."

A small boy with a burn scar across his cheek raised his hand tentatively. "Miss Wells—I mean, Mrs Thornton—what if we don't know what to write?"

Alice smiled, remembering her own first entries to Providence after her father's death. "Then you write exactly that, James. 'I don't know what to write.' And then perhaps the next line might come, and the next."

She moved between the desks, placing a journal before each child. When she reached Mary, the girl touched the leather cover with reverence.

"Is it truly mine to keep?" Mary whispered.

"Yes," Alice said, kneeling beside her desk. "Mrs Bennett's gift has provided for each of you to have one. Your words matter, Mary. They always have."

From the doorway, Alice sensed William watching. She glanced up to see him leaning against the frame, his eyes bright with pride. The headmaster's office behind him was modest—nothing like the grand studies of wealthy schools—but it was theirs, built on truth and sacrifice.

"Your stories are your own," Alice told the children, returning to the front of the room. "No one can take them from you. And when you write them down, they become a light that others might follow."

EPILOGUE

Alice settled herself on the bench in the small garden behind their school, adjusting her position to accommodate her growing belly. The late spring sunshine warmed her face as she unfolded Edgar's letter, smoothing the creases with careful fingers. Her other hand rested protectively over the swell of her child, due in less than two months.

My dear friends, Edgar had written in his precise hand, *London has proven to be everything I hoped for in terms of purpose, but it has given me something I never expected to find—love.*

Alice smiled, glancing up from the letter to watch William in the schoolyard. He stood beneath the old elm tree, surrounded by a circle of children—former factory workers whose small hands now held books instead of bobbins and whose faces turned up toward him with rapt attention.

. . .

Her name is Catherine Morris, Edgar's letter continued. *Her father runs a school for the children of dockhands, and she teaches there. We met at a committee meeting on educational reform, and I knew at once she possessed the same fire for justice that I've come to admire in both of you.*

The children's voices carried across the garden as they read aloud from the Book of Isaiah—"...and a little child shall lead them." William's patient corrections and gentle encouragement made Alice's heart swell with pride. How far they had come from those secret lessons beneath the oak tree at Pullman Manor.

We shall be married in the autumn, Edgar wrote. *I hope you both—the three of you by then—might attend. Catherine is eager to discuss your teaching methods, Alice. She believes your approach to the mill children could be adapted for the dockworkers' children as well.*

Alice folded the letter and tucked it into her pocket. The child within her stirred, a flutter of movement that still amazed her each time. She thought of how differently everything had turned out than she could have imagined that terrible night her father died. The pain remained, but it had transformed into something purposeful.

William looked up from his lesson and caught her eye across the yard. He smiled, that same smile that had first given her hope when she was invisible to everyone else at Pullman Manor.

Alice reached for her second leather-bound journal—William's gift from years ago—its pages now filled with multitudes of reflection, struggle, and ultimately, triumph. The leather was worn soft at the corners, bearing witness to countless nights of writing by candlelight. She opened to a fresh page, dipped her pen in ink, and paused, her free hand resting on the swell of her abdomen where their child grew.

The garden around her bloomed with forget-me-nots that Thomas had given her, now transplanted to this new beginning. She had planted them herself in the soil of their modest school garden, a reminder of endurance and hope.

Dear Providence, she began, then paused and added, *and dearest child yet to know this world.*

The words flowed from her pen with certainty, no longer the desperate questions of a grieving girl but the reflections of a woman who had walked through fire and emerged stronger.

Though the path that brought your father and me together was marked with fire and loss, I would walk it again without hesitation, for it was also lined with divine purpose. May you inherit your grandfather's courage, your father's compassion, and above all, the certainty that no darkness can extinguish the light of faith when it burns in a heart open to Providence's guidance.

Alice paused, watching as William dismissed his students for the afternoon. Their voices carried across the garden—children who once would have been bent over machines now reciting poetry and sums. She continued writing.

. . .

Through years of solitude, my words to you were my comfort. Now I write that you may one day understand: true romance is not found in ease or comfort, but in two souls recognising in each other the perfect companion for the work God has called them to do together.

William approached silently across the grass, his shadow falling across her page. He sat beside her on the bench, his presence as familiar and necessary as breath. He placed his hand gently over hers where it rested on her rounded abdomen, feeling the movement of their child beneath.

"May I?" he asked, gesturing to her journal.

Alice nodded and handed him the pages. William read her words aloud, his voice steady and warm in the afternoon light. When he finished, he leaned forward and pressed his lips to her forehead—the same spot where their love had first been acknowledged years before beneath the oak tree at Pullman Manor.

"Every prayer led us home," he whispered against her skin.

THE FIRST CHAPTER OF 'THE FORSAKEN LACEMAKER OF HAMPSTEAD'

Sunlight crept through the lace curtains, casting intricate shadows across Mabel's face. She blinked away sleep, watching the delicate patterns dance on the wooden floor of their cottage bedroom. The familiar shapes reminded her of the stories her mother wove into each design—flowers for hope, circles for eternity, leaves for growth.

The floorboards creaked beneath her feet as she slipped from beneath the warm quilts. Through the doorway, dried flowers hung in neat bundles from the kitchen rafters—purple lavender, white daisies, and golden yarrow. Their faded perfume mingled with the morning air. Mother's latest lace designs adorned the walls, each piece telling its own tale. A collar with intertwined roses spoke of summer gardens, while a shawl's pattern echoed the flight of swallows.

"Time to rise, sleepyhead," Mary called from the kitchen. The gentle clatter of dishes accompanied her voice.

Mabel selected a simple cotton dress from the chest, its fabric soft from many washings. She pulled it over her head, smoothing the wrinkles with practiced care. Though she was only nine, her fingers worked swiftly, separating her chestnut hair into three sections.

Mabel padded across the worn floorboards toward the kitchen, where her mother bent over her work table. Threads and bobbins scattered across its surface caught the morning light. The smell of fresh bread embraced her, mingling with the earthy scent of dried flowers and starched lace.

Her sister, Emma, sat at the corner of the table, her small tongue poking out in concentration as she traced flowers across the pages of her sketchbook. Her chubby five-year-old hands were surprisingly dexterous. Her bright blue eyes darted between the dried blooms hanging above and her emerging artwork. Her other sibling, Henry, squirmed in his chair beside her, more interested in creating towers from his wooden bowls than eating his breakfast.

Two-year-old Henry smacked two wooden bowels together in delight. Emma's musical giggle filled the air.

Mabel reached for the family's prized tablecloth, her fingers tracing the delicate pattern Mary had created for her wedding day. Each stitch told a story—lilies for love, roses for beauty, ivy for faithfulness. She spread it carefully across the table, smoothing away invisible wrinkles.

Thomas' heavy footsteps announced his arrival. He filled the doorway with his presence, already dressed for teaching in his well-worn but carefully pressed coat.

Thomas settled into his chair, his eyes twinkling as he cut into his bread. "You wouldn't believe what young Timothy did yesterday." He leaned forward, drawing the children closer with his conspiratorial tone. "He brought a frog to class, hidden in his slate."

Emma's eyes widened. "What happened next, Papa?"

"Well, this frog had quite different ideas about arithmetic. It hopped straight onto Miss Martha's copy book!"

Henry clapped his hands, spilling crumbs across the precious tablecloth. Mary reached over to brush them away, her fingers lingering on Thomas' sleeve. Their shared glance spoke volumes —years of love and understanding passing between them in a single moment.

After the plates were cleared, Mabel watched her father arrange his books on the kitchen table. His fingers traced the spines with reverence—Shakespeare, Milton, even a battered copy of Robinson Crusoe that had seen better days.

"The older students are ready for poetry," he mused, showing Mary a page marked with neat annotations. She nodded, suggesting passages that might capture young minds.

"What's this word mean?" Emma appeared at Thomas' elbow, pointing to a page in her own book. "'Mag-nif-i-cent'?"

"Ah!" Thomas' face lit up. "It means something grand and beautiful—like your mother's lace, or the sunset over Hampstead Heath."

Emma tried the word herself, stumbling over the syllables. Henry, watching from his perch on Mary's lap, waved his arms in imitation of her careful gestures, sending both siblings into fits of giggles.

Mabel's heart swelled as she watched her father guide Emma through the pronunciation. His patience never wavered, his joy in teaching as evident here at their kitchen table as it was in his classroom. In their modest cottage, filled with books and lace and love, she understood how knowledge could transform the simplest moments into something precious.

Click here to read the rest of
The Forsaken Lacemaker of Hampstead'

Artistry. Resilience. A Love That Defies Hardships.

In the shadow of Victorian London, Mabel Fairchild's life is shattered by false accusations and devastating loss. With two younger siblings dependent on her care, she makes an impossible promise: to keep her family together despite the world's cruel intentions.

Armed with nothing but her mother's lacemaking skills and unwavering determination, Mabel navigates the treacherous streets of London. Each delicate stitch she creates becomes both her survival and her art in a world that offers little mercy to those without means or name.

When fate leads her into service at the imposing Montague household, Mabel finds herself caught in a web of social expectations and hidden agendas. Her connection with Edward Montague, a young doctor with dreams of his own, threatens carefully laid plans and long-guarded secrets that powerful figures will stop at nothing to protect.

As illness and adversity test her resolve, Mabel must decide what sacrifices she's willing to make. Can she pursue both duty and desire? Will she dare to reach across the divide of class for a chance at happiness?

From the leafy lanes of Hampstead to the heart of Derby, Mabel's journey weaves together threads of injustice, ambition, and the delicate strength found in both lace and love. In a society that values station over character, can the fine patterns of truth finally emerge?

'The Forsaken Lacemaker of Hampstead'

without sex or swearing, but with all of the mystery and romance you expect from a great story.

Be the first to know when we release new books, take part in our fun competitions, and get surprise free books in your inbox by signing up to our free VIP Reader list.

As a thank you you'll receive a copy of 'The Little Orphan Waif's Crusade' straight away, alongside other gifts.

Click here to sign up for our mailing list, and receive your FREE stories.

CornerstoneTales.com/sign-up

LOVE VICTORIAN ROMANCE?

Other Rachel Downing Books

The Forsaken Lacemaker of Hampstead

In the shadow of Victorian London, Mabel Fairchild's life is shattered by false accusations and devastating loss. With two younger siblings dependent on her care, she makes an impossible promise: to keep her family together despite the world's cruel intentions.

Get 'The Forsaken Lacemaker of Hampstead' Here!

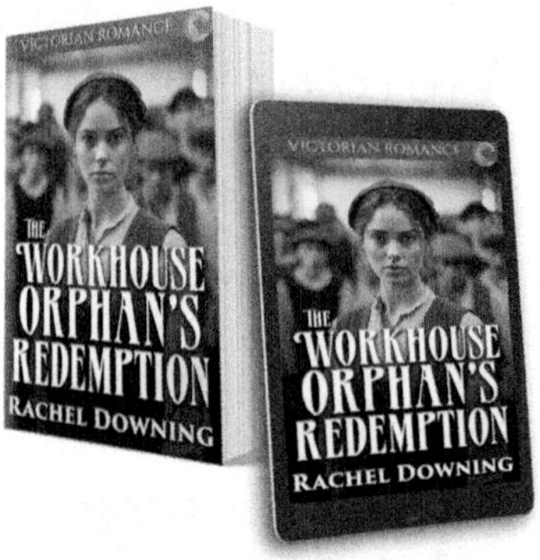

The Workhouse Orphan's Redemption

In the brutal world of Victorian London, Emma Redbrook's life begins in tragedy. Orphaned and trapped in Grimshaw's Workhouse, she endures cruelty that would break most spirits. But Emma's unwavering faith becomes her beacon of hope — and her strength.

Get 'The Workhouse Orphan's Redemption' Here!

The Orphan's Christmas Hymn

Seven-year-old Clara Winters' world shatters when tragedy strikes days before Christmas. Sent to St. Mary's Church Orphanage, she finds her only solace in the hymns that once filled her happy home. When her angelic voice catches the attention of the kind-hearted Reverend Thornton and his musically gifted son Edward, Clara dares to dream of a brighter future.

Get 'The Orphan's Christmas Hymn' Here!

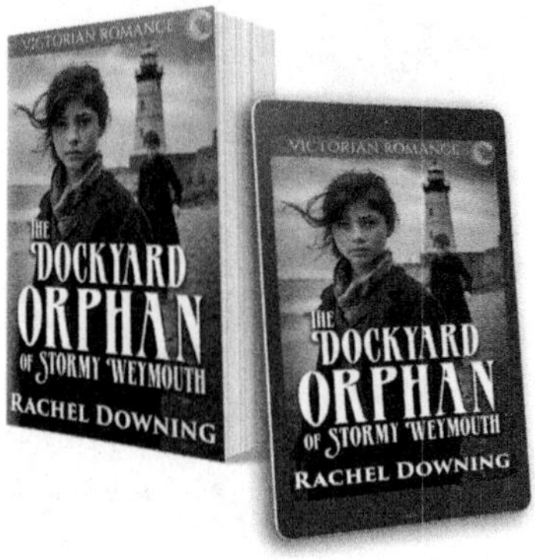

The Dockyard Orphan of Stormy Weymouth

Sarah Campbell's world crumbles when a tragic accident claims her parents' lives. She finds solace in the lighthouse's beam that guides ships to safety. But it's a young fisherman wrestling with his own loss, who truly captures her heart.

Get 'The Dockyard Orphan of Stormy Weymouth' Here!

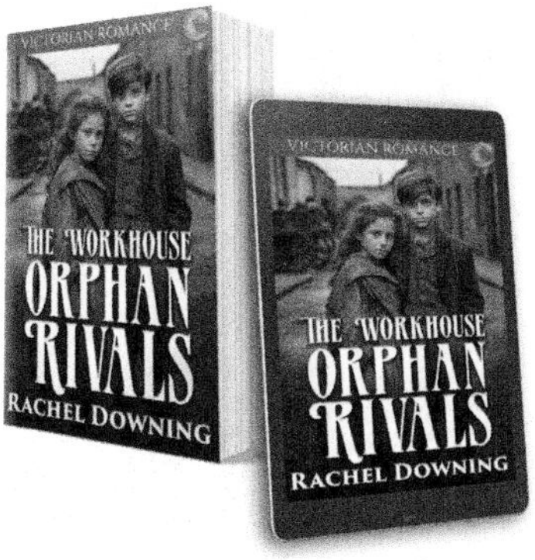

The Workhouse Orphan Rivals

Childhood sweethearts torn apart. A promise broken. A love that refuses to die.

Get 'The Workhouse Orphan Rivals' Here!

The Orphan Prodigy's Stolen Tale

When ten-year-old Isabella Farmerson's world shatters with the tragic loss of her parents, she's thrust into a life of hardship and uncertainty.

Get 'The Orphan Prodigy's Stolen Tale' Here!

The Lost Orphans of Dark Streets

Follow the stories of Elizabeth and Molly as they negotiate the dangerous slums and find their place in the world.

Get 'The Lost Orphans of Dark Streets' Here!

Two Steadfast Orphan's Dreams

Follow the stories of Isabella and Ada as they overcome all odds and find love.

Get 'Two Steadfast Orphan's Dreams' Here!

And from our other Victorian Romance Author Dorothy Wellings...

The Moral Maid's Unjust Trial

Matilda must fend for herself when her father is wrongfully accused for a crime he didn't commit.

Get 'The Moral Maid's Unjust Trial' Here!

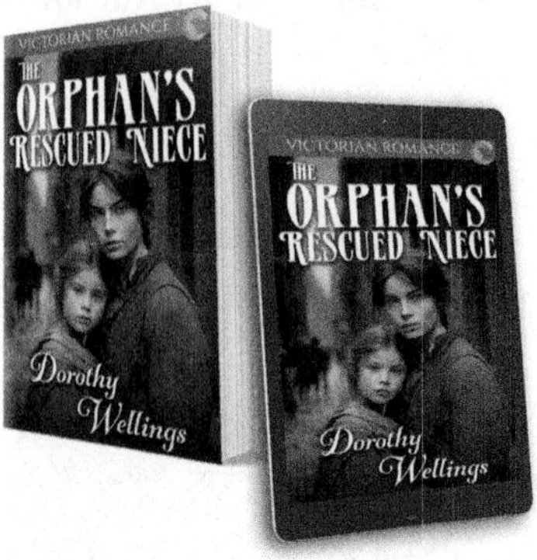

The Orphan's Rescued Niece

As Beatrice grows from a wide-eyed child into a resilient young woman, she finds herself caught between her love for her troubled brother and her desire for a life free from poverty and fear.

Get 'The Orphan's Rescued Niece' Here!

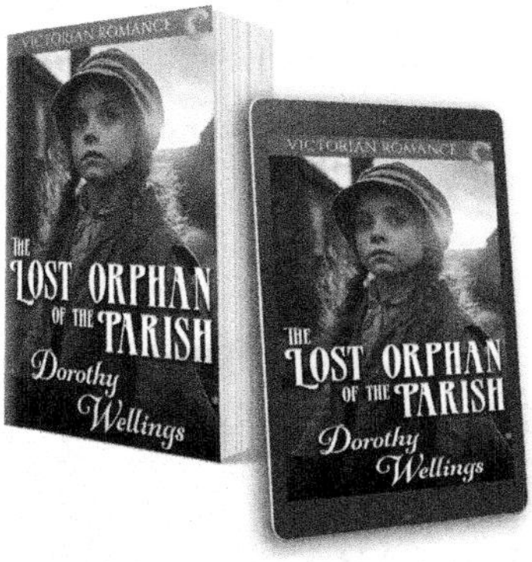

The Lost Orphan of the Parish

Annabelle's world shatters when illness claims her beloved parents. Left alone at ten years old with no inheritance, she's sent to the harsh Thornfield Orphanage with nothing but her father's worn Bible and the memories of his gentle teachings.

Get 'The Lost Orphan of the Parish' Here!

If you enjoyed this story, sign up to our mailing list to be the first to hear about our new releases and any sales and deals we have.

We also want to offer you a Victorian Romance novella - 'The Little Orphan Waif's Crusade' - absolutely free!

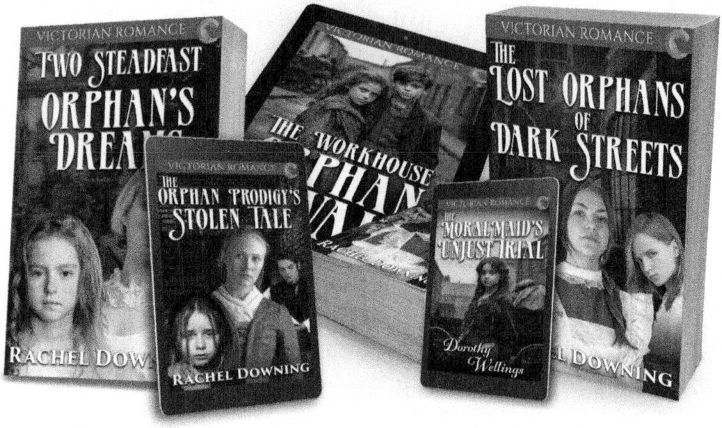

Click here to sign up for our mailing list, and receive your FREE stories.

CornerstoneTales.com/sign-up

Printed in Dunstable, United Kingdom

65524709R00119